THE GLENTHORNE

AND OTHER

LEOPARD

D0800535

Also by the author

THE PRIME MINISTERS OF CANADA

OLYMPIC VICTORY

LEOPARD IN THE AFTERNOON

THE MAN-EATER OF PUNANAI

SINDH REVISITED

JOURNEY TO THE SOURCE OF THE NILE

HEMINGWAY IN AFRICA

WOOLF IN CEYLON

THE POWER OF PAPER

THE GLENTHORNE CAT

AND OTHER AMAZING LEOPARD STORIES

COMPILED & EDITED BY

CHRISTOPHER ONDAATJE

HarperCollins*PublishersLtd*

The Glenthorne Cat
and other amazing leopard stories
© 2008 by Christopher Ondaatje.
All rights reserved.

Published by HarperCollins Publishers Ltd

First edition

HarperCollins books may be purchased for educational, business,
or sales promotional use through our Special Markets Department.

HarperCollins Publishers Ltd
2 Bloor Street East, 20th Floor
Toronto, Ontario, Canada
M4W 1A8

www.harpercollins.ca

Library and Archives Canada Cataloguing in Publication information is available.

ISBN: 978-1-55468-184-6

9 8 7 6 5 4 3 2 1

Photographs on pages 6, 8, 14, 18, 25, 30, 32, 34, 58, 62, 66, 68, 74, 81, 84, 95,
105, 119, 122, 131, 148,170, 183, 199, 217 copyright The Ondaatje Foundation.

Designed and typeset by Libanus Press, Marlborough, England
Printed and bound by Butler & Tanner, Frome

For Raj de Silva, Childers Jayawardhana
and Lakshman Senatilleke.
We have travelled many miles
and seen many leopards together.

Contents

Introduction

Leopards have fascinated Christopher Ondaatje for most of his life – ever since he saw his first cat in the Yala Game Sanctuary in Ceylon (now Sri Lanka) in 1946. He has also been quoted as having identified with them as predator rather than prey. I first met Ondaatje in 1996 when he had just completed his first speech at The Royal Geographical Society (with The Institute of British Geographers) on the early life of Sir Richard Burton, the great Victorian explorer, in Sindh. I remember him quoting the poet Wilfrid Blunt describing Burton in this way:

> *"His dress and appearance were those suggesting a released convict . . . a rusty black coat with a crumpled black silk stock, his throat destitute of collar, a costume which his muscular frame and immense chest made singularly and incongruously hideous, above it a countenance the most sinister I have ever seen, dark, cruel, treacherous, with eyes like a wild beast's. He reminded me of a black leopard, caged, but unforgiving . . ."*

Ondaatje was clearly under the spell of Burton. In many ways they are kindred spirits, and he gave a picture of the enigmatic restless explorer as few authors had given before. It wasn't surprising. His book *Sindh Revisited* was just out and Ondaatje had outlined his own incredible journey deep into the heart of British India, and the India and Sindh of today. The journey covered thousands of miles trekking across deserts where ancient peoples meet modern civilization on the banks of the mighty Indus River.

Since then I have got to know Ondaatje better. Like Burton he too has an insatiable restlessness and a quixotic, sometimes unfathomable, character akin to his beloved leopards. It is not surprising he has done this anthology. Let me quote from an earlier book of his *Leopard in the Afternoon*:

> *"A creature unique and paradoxical, sinister and ruthless, the leopard is at the same time charismatic and vulnerable."*

Here is another revealing quote:

> *"A leopard is smaller than a lion but can tear its prey apart with its hind legs while its sharp jaws lock into its victim's throat to strangle it. It is fierce and extremely dangerous when cornered."*

These are characteristics prevalent in all the twelve chapters chosen for this unique collection of leopard stories, old and new. Jim Corbett's famous "The Man-Eating Leopard of Rudraprayag" is included, as well as Balzac's classic "A Passion in the Desert". They are reminders of the heights that adventure writing can attain. Kenneth Anderson's two perilous experiences with leopards in South India are included, and a short but sensuous Burmese story by Anna Kavan is one that I had never read before. Finally, Christopher Ondaatje's own singularly curious "The Glenthorne Cat" evokes the greatest sense of mystery for me. It is a compelling story – sometimes gruesome, sometimes sympathetic, but cryptic and inscrutable.

I enjoyed this unusual book, despite the grisly interludes, because I too share a fascination for wild cats and love of good storytelling – not to mention the dramatic photographs, mostly taken by Ondaatje, that put him firmly across the danger line. Wildlife enthusiasts and hesitant explorers alike will find this an intriguing read. What an adventure, and what an experience!

Dr Rita Gardner, CBE
Director, Royal Geographical Society
(with I.B.G.)

Acknowledgements

For many years I have been urged to accumulate and tell the leopard stories in this book. They have been very much part of my life and I am eternally grateful to the people who have helped me to bring it about. "A Visit" by Anna Kavan from *Julia and the Bazooka* is reproduced with permission of Peter Owen Ltd., London; "The Man-Eating Leopard of Rudraprayag" by Jim Corbett is reproduced by permission of Oxford University Press, India, New Delhi; and Kenneth Anderson's "The Black Panther of Sivanipalli" and "The Man-Eating Panther of the Yellagiri Hills" are reproduced by permission of Rupa Publishing, India. The cover photograph and black leopard photographs on pages 12, 102 and 113 are reproduced with permission of Alan & Sandy Carey/Still Pictures; and the photograph of the black leopard on page 136 is reproduced by permission of Andy Rouse.

Finally I am grateful to Dinny Gollop, Nick Smith and Susan Dyer for their invaluable help in preparing parts of this manuscript; and to Michael Berry and Michael Mitchell who helped with the book's design and production. Without them it would have been almost impossible to have produced this book.

CHAPTER 1

The Glenthorne Cat

CHRISTOPHER ONDAATJE

*The first rumours started in the late 1970s and reached a
fever pitch in 1983, when eighty sheep were found dead,
their throats ripped out and their skin torn by claw marks.
At about the same time, local farmers started reporting
sightings of large cat-like creatures with black or dark grey
fur, a long tail and green eyes, which stood low to the
ground. Reports mushroomed and were taken so seriously
that, in 1988, the then Ministry of Agriculture, Fisheries
and Food sent in a party of Royal Marines to carry out a
search. Nothing was found, however, but the claw marks on
the trees abutting the coastal path above and west of
Glenthorne were confirmed to have been made by a large
cat, probably a leopard.*

All my life I have felt that the wildness of the world is never that far away.
From the freedom of my early childhood in Ceylon to the stuffy board-
rooms of the Canadian business world, I have sensed the nearness of the
wild, in nature and in people too. In recent years, freed from the world
of business, I have been able not just to sense the proximity of the wild,
but to set out to reach it. I have found it in the disappearing tail of a
leopard I have been tracking for days, in the impossible promise of an
African plain at first light, in the stripped carcass of a buffalo left to
stink in the sun. But I have also known since childhood that it is not

necessary to travel to exotic climes to find wildness. Even today, driving out of London, as the neon glow of the city filters further and further into the country night sky and the reassuring drone of the motorway seems constant, it is not so long a road to find silence and disconcerting darkness. It is still not so far from suburbia to landscapes that mock our attempts at cosy civilisation and can fill the modern, cynical spirit with wonder. My home, Glenthorne, is set in just such a place.

Glenthorne itself is the product of a true Romantic imagination. In 1831, in his own attempt to reconcile the civilised and the sublime, the Reverend Walter S. Halliday chose to build his house on an almost sheer North Devon cliff. One of the most awkward and inconvenient settings in England, it is also one of the most spectacular. At first sight, the house seems to stand in marvellous isolation; the surrounding hills are so

The Reverend Walter
S. Halliday, 1794–1872

thickly wooded that it is hard to make out the three mile drive that careens through hairpin bends and down a thousand feet to the only piece of flat land between Porlock and Lynmouth. At the front of the house, the lawn drops away precipitously into the sea and the view from the terrace answers the Devon coastline with thirteen miles of sea and the Welsh cliffs. This view opens out onto wide sky and the power of the sea, but the back of the house is shelved in tight. The chimneys reach only as high as the winding roots of the trees that climb the giant hills behind, and the dense woods themselves, separated only by steep smugglers' paths and narrow streams, cast the back of the house into darkness.

Halliday's vision of the picturesque did not seek to set man's achievements on an equal footing with nature and the comparative modesty of his architecture is overpowered by the magnificence of the landscape. In winter, the high hills triumph even over the sun, which does not rise high enough to let light drift down into the house. In winter, Glenthorne's romance is suffused with gloom and an atmosphere of mystery pervades the place. It was on such a February day, many years ago, that I first saw the house. Perhaps I should have known, even then, that its strangeness would draw me back.

I grew up in the Exmoor[1] countryside around Glenthorne. I had been sent out from Ceylon to England by my parents to get a decent education at Blundell's School in Tiverton. It was a tough place, its strictures and traditions as alien to my understanding at first as were the bleak expanses of moorland and heather to my eye. I spent a considerable time learning the ways and manners of an English public school and I spent time adjusting to my natural surroundings too. In the holidays I would set

---

1 The boundaries of Exmoor were created in 1954 when the Exmoor National Park was established. The Park measures 32 miles from west to east, and almost 14 miles from north to south. The total area is about 160,000 acres, or about 265 square miles. One third of the park lies in Devon, and two thirds in Somerset; the northern boundary is the southern coast of the Bristol Channel stretching from Combe Martin in the west to Minehead in the east.

out from the tiny village of Timberscombe where I was living with my uncle, ignoring the tasteful, pink sandstone houses and carefully tended gardens, drawn by the moors, the intense green of the combes and the sweep of the hills down to the sea. On one such adventure, I stumbled across the remote dirt track that led to Glenthorne. I hurried along the zig-zagging path far enough to get a clear view of the shadowy house and gazed a long time, enjoying the slight shiver of mystery I felt in its presence. But I trespassed no further. Exmoor is rife with tales of curses, withcraft and the supernatural and I had heard the rumours that people who ventured uninvited into the house seldom returned. With that thought in mind I turned back along the long drive, scrambling north up the steep slope along one of the old smugglers' paths and dashing along the coastal path, oblivious in my haste to the strange markings on one of the trees that lined the route.

This is Lorna Doone country. It was of this area that R. D. Blackmore wrote his great romantic tale *Lorna Doone*,[2] in 1869. Yenworthy, the Ridd Farm, towers above Glenthorne to the east, and the much-visited Oare Church, where the wicked Carver Doone shot Lorna on her wedding day, lies only a few miles 'up over' in the village of Oare, a few yards from the River Lyn.

It was twenty-eight years before I felt that particular shiver of excitement again. Just before my last year at Blundell's I received a letter from my mother telling me that I could not continue at school because there was no more money. I had no idea of the family's financial troubles. Like most privileged children, I did not entertain such thoughts. After my long acclimatisation, things had been finally going well at school and now I would have to leave without experiencing life in the upper sixth

---

2 *Lorna Doone, A Romance of Exmoor*, is a novel by Richard Doddridge Blackmore. It was first published anonymously in 1869, in a limited three-volume edition of just 500 copies, of which only 300 sold. The following year it was published in one volume and became a huge critical and financial success. It has never been out of print.

forms. Blundell's had become my second home and, in some ways, the shock of being forced out was more brutal than that of being sent away from Ceylon. Now penniless, I had to leave the comparative haven of an English public school and spent my seventeenth birthday in the City of London learning the intricacies of finance that would hold me in good stead in my pioneering business life in Canada, where I went in 1956. Canada was the land of my success, where I rebuilt my family's fortunes, but Ceylon and Exmoor, the wild places of my childhood from where I had been torn into adulthood, never left me.

And then in 1984, on my first visit to Blundell's after nearly three decades, I heard that Glenthorne was for sale. In the summer sunshine, the dilapidated old house looked much less forbidding to my adult eyes, but the atmosphere of mystery remained. That familiar sense of excitement and strangeness returned. I was warned that the house was virtually in ruins but this did not dissuade me or – eventually – my wife. Nor, this time, did the old rumours about the house – which surfaced in conversation as strongly as ever.

Outside Glenthorne, in the locality, there remains a whole host of superstitions and, although people today adopt a rather contemptuous attitude to the old sayings and practices, they are far from forgotten. E. W. Hendy, the author of *Wild Exmoor through the Year*, tells us that village herbalists have been known to use the juice of celandine to cure certain physical afflictions. A black slug smeared on a wart and then placed on a thorn somehow gets rid of the nasty growth. A sty can be treated if a woman passes her wedding ring over it four times from right to left. You can keep a witch away by driving a nail into her footprint. You can always tell the number of years before you will be married by hanging a sheep's heart in your house and counting the drops of blood that drip from it. Never burn old love letters . . . it is unlucky. If a door refuses to remain closed, it is a warning of imminent death. Keep a donkey among your cows to keep off witches.

But of all Exmoor's superstitions, the most famous, feared and

In 1831 the Reverend Walter S. Halliday chose to build his house on an almost sheer North Devon cliff.

ridiculed is the Beast of Exmoor.[3] Tales of the beast are usually – understandably – met with raised eyebrows and sceptical retorts but Exmoor is an ideal habitat for predators. There is no doubt either, having explored my boyhood escape route many times and much more closely, that one of the trees on the coastal path immediately above Glenthorne bears the claw marks, about six feet up, of a large cat – similar to the territorial markings of a leopard.

This time, I would not be deterred by rumour and superstition. I hired a lawyer in nearby Minehead and paid the asking price for the ruined building. During the next year, while we were still living in Canada, my wife and I painstakingly restored Glenthorne from an early 19th-century print of the house, which we found in an antique shop in Lynton. We repaired the Delabole[4] slate roof, the Gothic spires and the broken Bath stone balustrades, and decorated the many rooms and corridors of the building as near as we could to the comfortable Victorian glory of its prime. It was a tireless task for we left few displaced stones unturned. We read and learned our history, closely researching the Halliday family and the story of the house. It seemed only right in our restorations to pay particular attention to the magnificent library on the ground floor and the first floor study of the Reverend Walter S. Halliday, himself so much a reclusive bibliophile.

3 There have been several sightings of black panthers on Exmoor, even in the past few years. In 2001 the Spanish maid at Oare Manor told her employers, Mr & Mrs Nicholas Browne, that she had seen a large black cat at dusk immediately outside her bedroom window and trying to enter the chicken coop. The cat was seen again the next night again attempting to get at the chickens. Then, later that week, the creature was seen straddling the limb of a tree overhanging the Lyn River near Brendon by a fisherman. This was also at dusk. *Country Life* reported on 25 September 2002 that 'a dark shape some five foot long, crouched over the top of a hedge, green eyes glaring at the truck which dared to be in its way. The driver moved back up the slope to get a better look, but the animal disappeared in the shadows. It was May 2002 and it was the latest sighting of the Beast of Exmoor.'

4 The Delabole slate quarry in North Cornwall is one of the largest of its type in England and has run continuously since the 15th century.

During the next five years, even though we stayed at Glenthorne for the occasional extended holiday, introducing this romantic place to our children and some of our more intrepid friends, we continued to live in Canada. But then, by the end of 1988, disillusioned with the North American financial scene with its ever-growing responsibilities, and feeling the old longing for *Lorna Doone* country, we sold our house in Toronto, moved to a flat on Sloane Square in London and determined to spend more time at Glenthorne. It is an enigmatic place, and we had to learn how to handle this grand old lady that we bought and gradually come to love. It wasn't easy. Glenthorne is not everyone's cup of tea, as we learned. It had to like you too and we always felt, as we still do today, that even though we owned Glenthorne, that the house was still very much the domain of the Reverend Halliday – although he had died in 1872.

His presence felt so strong that I began to suspect there might have been some truth in the rumours of ghosts at Glenthorne. It seemed that he was always around. When we hung some old hunting prints in the back hall, the oldest part of the house, one hunting scene was later found to have been hurled far across the hall, and the substantial nail which we had hammered into the wall was bent double. None of the windows or doors had been opened. We hung the old print in another, less conspicuous place and apparently this was deemed acceptable – the print was left untouched. Similarly, when we installed a radio and tape player into the downstairs library, the panelled door to the oval room, walled with books, banged constantly for nearly ten minutes. Again none of the windows or other doors were opened and my wife, the engineer and I watched the door in amazement. However, we left the radio-tape player in place, hidden between leather bound books, and we didn't have any more trouble from the understandably irritated old man. His presence was strongest at night or in the early hours of the morning, especially in his study on the first floor overlooking the old croquet lawn and eastwards down the steep cliffs and the Bristol Channel. We often heard him, but we never saw him.

That is, until that one cold December night last year when I was battling with my *Woolf in Ceylon* manuscript. The aim of the book was to trace the journey and seven years that Leonard Woolf spent in Ceylon from 1904–11 as a young British civil servant, and I had just come back from the Hambantota district on the south-east coast where Woolf served as assistant government agent. Although I didn't know it at the time, it was only five days before the catastrophic tsunami[5] struck the island, as it did many other countries in South East Asia. As I said, I was struggling with my manuscript, trying to interweave Woolf's career in Ceylon with some social commentary on what had happened to Ceylon after Woolf, and particularly after independence in 1948. I was tired. The words began to blur in front of my eyes. Thinking of going to bed, I settled down in my favourite armchair, closed my eyes for only a second and suddenly realised that there was another presence in the room.

When I looked up there was an old gentleman, well wrapped up in a scarf and nightgown, seated in a chair a short distance away from me. He was looking at me quizzically. It never occurred to me to be frightened – it was quite clear who this must be, the stubborn chin and dreamer's eyes familiar from portraits around the house. Perhaps because we had lived with his presence for so long, it felt oddly natural that he should appear now, comfortably settled in his much-loved study and speaking in a low, courteous voice, "I see that you're writing a book about Ceylon."

"I am, sir," I replied, "and I'm not having an easy time of it."

There was a pause. The old Reverend seemed to be looking me up and down, trying to decide whether to continue. I held my breath, fearing that he would disappear as suddenly as he had arrived.

---

5 The 2004 Indian Ocean earthquake or 'Boxing Day Tsunami', known by the scientific community as the Sumatra-Andaman earthquake, was an undersea earthquake that occurred on 26 December 2004. The earthquake triggered a series of devastating tsunamis along the coasts of most landmasses bordering the Indian Ocean, killing large numbers of people and inundating coastal communities across South and South-East Asia, including parts of India, Indonesia, Sri Lanka and Thailand.

"You know," he said, eventually breaking the silence, "You're not the first person from Ceylon to have lived or stayed at Glenthorne."

"I know, sir. I have been told that Samuel Baker[6], who spent some years in Ceylon, used to come down here in the 1870's after his discovery of Lake Albert."

The old man smiled as if remembering some long past mischief. "Yes. Sam was a good friend. He came to stay with his Hungarian wife several times. Always full of outrageous stories and adventures. She was quite a woman too. Bought her out of a slave market in Turkey and she stuck with him through all his Nile adventures. Lots of fun.

"But it wasn't Sam Baker that I am speaking of. Did you know that a friend of my family – actually a friend of my sister's son – also went out to Ceylon and lived there for a while before he came back to England and lived here at Glenthorne? I say he lived here, and he did, but only for a few months because he got involved in . . . in something so strange I have never spoken of it before. But you, I have noticed your interest in such things – ever since you were a boy too scared to come to Glenthorne's door. Perhaps you might believe me."

My mind was still racing when the Reverend startled me with his next question.

"What do you know about the cat people of Ceylon?"

The cat people of Ceylon? I have always been fascinated with mythology, and indeed witchcraft and superstition, as Halliday seemed to know, but I had never heard of cat people in connection with Ceylon. Still, my curiosity led me on – perhaps if I told what I could remember from the *Mahavansa*, the chronicle of the Sinhalese, my ghostly visitor would continue with his own story.

"Well, Sir, I do know that the beginnings of Ceylon remain in the realm

---

6 Sir Samuel White Baker (1821–93) wrote two books about Sri Lanka, *The Rifle and the Hound in Ceylon* (1853) and *Wanderings in Ceylon* (1855). He is recorded as having bought his second wife Barbara Maria Szasz at a white slave auction, which is said to be the principal reason why Queen Victoria refused to meet Baker.

of myth and have their links with cats, in a way. The stories I've been told, and read in a translation of the *Mahavansa*, tell of the daughter of the king of Kalinga, a beautiful girl with a passionate character – so much so that her parents were ashamed of her lustful nature. Walking in the wilderness one day, she was approached by a lion prowling for his prey; far from being terrified, she caressed and excited him. The lion placed her on his back and carried her back to his den. It is said that the twins who resulted from this strange union bore the lion's paws in place of their hands and feet. Is that the story you are talking about?" I asked the Reverend.

"Sort of. What else do you know?"

"Well, from what I can remember, the twins grew up and escaped and the son, Sihabahu, eventually killed his lion father in return for a reward of three thousand pieces of gold from the local king. When the king died, the young man succeeded him."

I felt quite proud of myself remembering all this but the Reverend, seemed unimpressed and gestured impatiently for me to continue.

"Sihabahu founded a city called Sihaparu and went on to sire sixteen sets of twins. The eldest twin was called Vijaya but Vijaya grew up to be a lawless character, a violent ruffian. The king banished his son for his riotous ways and sent him into exile in a rudderless boat. Eventually, when he had reformed his ways and gained the wisdom of experience, he landed at Tambapanni – later called Taprobane, the old name for Ceylon. Vijaya is the founder of the Sinhalese race, so I suppose cats play a part in the mythology of the Sinhalese people . . . but I know nothing of any tales of cat people in Sri Lanka, or Ceylon as it was."

I stopped there, confused as to what the old man wanted me to know, or to tell him. There was another weighty silence where again it seemed that he was debating whether to tell his own story. By now, I was so curious it was all I could do not to prompt him to speak but I kept quiet and soon enough he began.

He spoke now in a very soft, deep voice to me. I had to strain to catch his words, and the amazing story he had to relate.

"As I told you, my nephew's friend – and I had better not give you his name, for obvious reasons – spent some time in Ceylon working in Colombo but also up-country in Nuwara Eliya and a place called Bogawantelawa on the Glencairn tea estate. You have probably been there. He was very taken by the country and by the people – particularly the Sinhalese who he thought were sensitive, creative, and extremely nice to him. He became very friendly with an aristocratic Kandyan family and, not surprisingly, as he spent a great deal of time with them – they were neighbours of his on the Glencairn estate – he met and fell in love with the daughter, Kumari. He told me later, after . . . when he had lost all his happiness, that it was her air of independence that attracted him first. More used to shy, milk-sop English girls, he was captivated by her assured manner – the proud tilt of her chin, the warmth of her smile. He admitted to me then that he left their very first meeting dreaming of her amber-flecked eyes and determined to win her love.

"Despite the disapproval of his family, he married his young bride in a secret Buddhist ceremony in Ceylon and brought her back to England less than six months later to live here at Glenthorne. He had, by then, fallen out with his family. We didn't know it then, but almost from the outset, despite the obvious love the young couple had for each other, the marriage ran into some trouble. Of course, none of us had any idea what the matter was, but there was a strained existence which none of us understood – least of all my young guest. Kumari's anxiety seemed to stem from something more profound than the understandable difficulties of moving to a cold, damp climate and a world far from home. She would alternate between clinging to her husband's side, hardly able to bear being away from him, to spending solitary hours roaming the moorland and the beach. For all that she adored him, she inflicted isolation and pain on them both.

Incredibly, she feared she was a direct descendant of a family whose ancestors had originally been conceived by the relationship between a human being and a cat.

"It was a difficult time for all of us in the house and we went to some considerable ends to keep the entire situation secret among members of our immediate family only. Certainly none of our neighbours knew anything– not even that the young man had brought back a wife from Ceylon. It was only by chance that one night, actually in this very room, he came to me in a terrible state and told me that despite the great love he and Kumari shared, the marriage had never been consummated."

Halliday explained that he tried to reason with the young man, and had eventually coaxed out of him the incredible truth, which she had only just explained to him, that Kumari feared that she was in fact the direct descendant of a family whose ancestors had originally been conceived by the relationship between a human being and a cat, and that there always had been a danger that any female member of the family, if sexually aroused, could turn into a giant cat.

I didn't say anything. It was an incredible story but I knew better than to express knee-jerk disbelief. I have seen enough inexplicable things, heard enough strange tales, than to scoff at this. But why was the old man telling me this story? And why now? What more did he have to tell me? The Reverend seemed in no particular hurry to continue. He looked at me searchingly. I dared not take my eyes off his for fear of breaking the spell, and for fear that he might stop, or go away forever. But I didn't ask the question I was dying to ask, "What happened next?" In time the Reverend spoke again – softly, deliberately, and with purpose.

"There was nothing I could do to reassure my young friend. He was inconsolable. We talked into the night and I did my best to convince him that tales of the supernatural and stories of myth and superstition were seldom true. And equally, being a man of the cloth, I didn't believe in weird transformations of man and beast. I tried also to allay his fears that Kumari must be unsound in mind to think such things. I suggested that the move from Ceylon to England could have stirred up many deep and confused thoughts about her heritage, her identity. My advice to him was to somehow try to dispel his young bride's fears and beliefs and to give her all the warmth and comfort she so obviously needed in this awful predicament that faced her. In time, I felt sure, that her fears would be overcome – and the two young people would live a normal and happy life.

"I wasn't sure if my talk had any effect, but for the next few weeks at least the strained situation continued. Nothing more was said and he didn't try to discuss the situation with me again. I presumed he was doing the best he could, and perhaps he was embarrassed by the earlier scene. The young couple came down to meals together, walked sometimes hand in hand around the gardens, and sometimes hiked up the smugglers' paths that wind up the combes to the windy heights of Exmoor. If one didn't know the awful truth one would suspect that what we were witnessing was a young couple very much in love, and very content in their own company. I began to feel more relaxed.

"However, I have always found that one feels most secure just before a storm. And so it was that one summer night in July, I was awakened sometime soon after midnight by my young friend in a state of great agitation.

"'She's gone,'" he told me.

"What do you mean?" I asked, still not fully awake and not wanting to believe what I was hearing. He started to tell me, haltingly at first, but soon caught up in his own memory of the night, oblivious to the unseemliness of his words.

"'Something strange happened. We were asleep in our bedroom down the hall when quite suddenly I woke up in Kumari's arms. She had been crying. I could taste her tears on her cheek. But she clung to me as if her very life depended on me. I must say that at that moment I loved her as much as I have ever loved her. We held each other close, neither one of us wanting to release the other. I must say I wanted her terribly, but didn't dare make a move knowing her fear. But she somehow seemed released of any of the superstition that had been tormenting her. She seemed free and different, almost happy – although I could still feel her wet cheeks.

And her arms still clung tightly around me. She was a different person – vibrant, sensual – the passionate being I always knew and hoped she would be. We were one and I knew then that she wanted me as I wanted her. Her breathing became faster. I felt her body arch and quiver and her head force itself under mine. Out of control, her passion appeared to have no boundaries. Writhing beneath me, still quivering in her nakedness, she suddenly screamed, still gripping me tightly, "Oh no. No. Not now. Not yet." And then breaking herself away from me, almost violently, she was gone into the night. I couldn't see her, and I couldn't stop her. I've been outside searching the bushes around the house, and even walked the length of the Water Garden. The almost-full moon would have allowed me to see anyone – but I saw nothing. Nothing. It's a warm night – but she has no clothes on and I'm afraid she'll catch her death of cold.'

"At that point, he broke down completely, but I immediately summoned the servants and housemaid and, with lanterns, all of us searched the grounds almost until dawn. We found no trace of the young woman, even though we scoured every inch of the grounds, down to and up the length of the stream and the Water Garden. We even walked the track to Home Farm, up to the Walled Garden and down the cliff path again to the house. We found and saw nothing and, knowing that we could do no more until morning, we retired to bed."

"And did you find her?" I asked anxiously.

The Reverend looked at me for the longest time before answering.

"No. The servants woke me the next morning and took me to a broken window in the front hall, which in our haste to get outside, we had completely missed the night before. The wood and the panes had been shattered, and there were scratch marks on the window sill and on the broken frame. Outside the window, on the ground, were the pug marks that seemed to have been made by some large cat-like animal. We tried to follow them, but only saw faint traces away from the house and up into the beech wood above the road. I never told this news to my young friend, fearing for his state of mind. Of course, we reported the situation to the Countisbury Constabulary, who organised further search parties over the next few days to cover the hills and woods around and behind Glenthorne, and also in the combes leading to Yenworthy and the valleys leading from the old Roman barrow near the coastal road. No one ever found any trace of the young woman. My friend was reconciled with his family in Yorkshire and I never heard from him again."

Again I waited, wondering if the Reverend would voice the impossible conclusion to which he seemed to be heading. But he only hinted at such a thought – true to the atmosphere of mystery at Glenthorne.

"So there's something for you to think about. You and I both know that there have been sightings of a large black cat from time to time on Exmoor, and there are clear territorial claw markings undoubtedly made by some member of the leopard family on the trees that line the coastal path from Glenthorne up to Countisbury. You have probably already noticed them. I don't think anyone has come to any clear conclusion about these cats – but they are definitely around and occasionally have been seen. But then no one knows this story. Why should they? It has been kept a secret among our two families for these many years. Why don't you put it down sometime? Perhaps, with a bit of extra research you might be able to shed a little more light on a disturbing event that happened a very long time ago.

"And now I must leave you – I hope you are enjoying my house. It is a strange place but I was very happy here. I hope you will be too."

And with that parting sentence, the Reverend simply took his leave. It was not a dramatic exit. He just wasn't there any more. I was alone again – with my thoughts and my story. It doesn't explain everything. But it does, as the Reverend so aptly put it, give us something to think about.

CHAPTER 2

A Visit

(from *Julia and the Bazooka*)

ANNA KAVAN

Anna Kavan died on 4th December 1968, putatively of heart failure, but, actually as a result of a lifetime's addiction to heroin. She had been preparing to inject herself with a shot that was still in the barrel of the syringe when she died. The plunger had not been depressed and she collapsed with the needle in her arm. She had a long history of attempted suicide and a propensity as a serious user to overdose. Kavan was a gifted writer and a talented painter who endured an unhappy childhood, two failed marriages and a long mutually dependent relationship with her psychiatrist. She began writing during her short-lived and explosive marriage to her alcoholic first husband who took her to Burma. Wishing in later life to eliminate entirely the facts of her past, Anna Kavan destroyed everything she had recorded about her troubled life including almost all of her personal correspondence and her diaries.

One hot night a leopard came into my room and lay down on the bed beside me. I was half asleep, and did not realize at first that it was a leopard. I seemed to be dreaming the sound of some large, soft-footed creature padding quietly through the house, the doors of which were wide open because of the intense heat. It was almost too dark to see the lithe, muscular shape coming into my room treading softly on velvet paws, coming straight to the bed without hesitation, as if perfectly familiar with its position.

A light spring, then warm breath on my arm, on my neck and shoulder, as the visitor sniffed me before lying down. It was not until later, when moonlight entering through the window revealed an abstract spotted design, that I recognized the form of an unusually large, handsome leopard stretched out beside me.

His breathing was deep though almost inaudible. He seemed to be sound asleep. I watched the regular contractions and expansions of the

I watched the regular contractions and expansions of the deep chest, admired the elegant relaxed body and supple limbs, and was confirmed in my conviction that the leopard is the most beautiful of all wild animals . . .

deep chest, admired the elegant relaxed body and supple limbs, and was confirmed in my conviction that the leopard is the most beautiful of all wild animals . . . While I observed him, I was all the time breathing his natural odour, a wild primeval smell of sunshine, freedom, moon and crushed leaves, combined with the cool freshness of the spotted hide, still damp with the midnight moisture of jungle plants. I found his non-human scent, surrounding him like an aura of strangeness, peculiarly attractive and stimulating.

My bed, like the walls of the house, was made of palm-leaf matting stretched over short bamboos, smooth and cool to the touch, even in the great heat. It was not so much a bed as a room within a room, an open staging about twelve feet square, so there was ample space for the leopard as well as myself. I slept better that night than I had since the hot weather started, and he too seemed to sleep peacefully at my side.

The close proximity of this powerful body of another species gave me a pleasant sensation that I am at a loss to name.

When I awoke in the faint light of dawn, with the parrots screeching outside, he had already got up and left the room.

CHAPTER 3

The Man-Eating Leopard of Rudraprayag

JIM CORBETT

Jim Corbett was born in 1875 and grew up in Kaldbung and Nainital in the then United Province of India. He was one of ten children who mixed freely with Indian children, becoming fluent in local dialects. It was during his twenty-year assignment as a trans-shipment inspector on the railways that he became hugely popular as a hunter of man-eaters. After years of following them he developed a great appreciation of how clever and cunning these animals can be. Corbett left India in 1947 after the British vacated India. He moved to Kenya. There he wrote six books about his experiences, one of which "The Man-Eating Leopard of Rudraprayag" was published in 1948. Corbett died in Kenya in 1955.

'Prayag' is the Hindi word for 'confluence'. At Rudraprayag, two rivers – the Mandakini coming down from Kedarnath, and the Alaknanda from Badrinath – meet, and from here onwards the combined waters of the two rivers are known to all Hindus as Ganga Mai, and to the rest of the world as the Ganges.

When an animal, be it a leopard or be it a tiger, becomes a man-eater, it is given a place-name for purposes of identification. The name so given to a man-eater does not necessarily imply that the animal began its man-eating career at, or that its kills were confined to, that particular place. It is quite natural that the leopard which started its man-eating career at a village twelve miles from Rudraprayag, on the Kedarnath pilgrim route, should have been known for the rest of its career as the Man-Eating Leopard of Rudraprayag.

Leopards do not become man-eaters for the same reasons tigers do. Though I hate to admit it, our leopards – the most beautiful and the most graceful of all the animals in our jungles, and who when cornered or wounded are second to none in courage – are scavengers to the extent that they will, when driven by hunger, eat any dead thing they find in the jungle, just as lions will in the African bush.

The people of Garhwal are Hindus, and as such cremate their dead. The cremation invariably takes place on the bank of a stream or river in order that the ashes may be washed into the Ganges and eventually into the sea. As most of the villages are situated high up on the hills, while the streams of rivers are in many cases miles away down in the valleys, it will be realised that a funeral entails a considerable tax on the man-power of a small community when, in addition to the carrying party, labour has to be provided to collect and carry the fuel needed for the cremation. In normal times these rites are carried out very effectively; but when disease in epidemic form sweeps through the hills, and the inhabitants die faster than can be disposed of, a very simple rite, which consists of placing a live coal in the mouth of the deceased, is performed in the village, and the body is then carried to the edge of the hill and cast into the valley below.

A leopard, in an area where its natural food is scarce, finding these bodies, very soon acquires a taste for human flesh, and when the disease dies down and normal conditions are re-established, he, very naturally, on finding his food supply cut off, takes to killing human beings. In the wave of the epidemic influenza that swept through the country in 1918 and cost India over a million lives, Garhwal suffered very severely, and it was at the end of this epidemic that the Garhwal man-eater made his appearance.

The first human kill accredited to the man-eating leopard of Rudraprayag is recorded as having taken place at Bainji village on 9 June 1918, and the last kill for which the man-eater was responsible took place in the Bhainswara village on 14 April 1926. Between these two dates the number of human kills recorded by Government was one hundred and twenty-five.

*   *   *

The word 'terror' is so generally and universally used in connection with everyday trivial matters that it is apt to fail to convey, when intended to do so, its real meaning. I should like therefore to give you some idea of what terror – real terror – meant to the fifty thousand inhabitants living in the five hundred square miles of Garhwal in which the man-eater was operating, and to the sixty thousand pilgrims who annually passed through the area between the years 1918 and 1926.

A boy, an orphan aged fourteen, was employed to look after a flock of forty goats. He was of the depressed – untouchable – class, and each evening when he returned with his charges he was given his food and then shut into a small room with the goats. The room was on the ground floor of a long row of double-storeyed buildings and was immediately below the room occupied by the boy's master, the owner of the goats. To prevent the goats crowding in on him as he slept, the boy had fenced off the far left-hand corner of the room.

The room had no windows and only one door, and when the boy and the goats were safely inside, the boy's master pulled the door to, and fastened it by pulling a hasp, which was attached by a short length of chain to the door, over the staple fixed in the lintel. A piece of wood was then inserted in the staple to keep the hasp in place, and on his side of the door the boy, for his better safety, rolled a stone against it.

On the night the orphan was gathered to his fathers, his master asserts the door was fastened as usual, and I have no reason to question the truth of his assertion. In support of it, the door showed many deep claw marks, and it is possible that in his attempts to claw open the door the leopard displaced the piece of wood that was keeping the hasp in place, after which it would have been easy for him to push the stone aside and enter the room.

Forty goats packed into a small room, one corner of which was fenced off, could not have left the intruder much space to manoeuvre in, and it is left to conjecture whether the leopard covered the distance from the door to the boy's corner of the room over the backs of the goats or under their bellies, for at this stage of the proceedings all the goats must have been on their feet.

It were best to assume that the boy slept through all the noise the leopard must have made when trying to force open the door, and that the goats must have made when the leopard had entered the room, and that he did not cry for help to deaf ears, only screened from him and the danger that menaced him by a thin plank.

After killing the boy in the fenced-off corner, the leopard carried him across the empty room – the goats had escaped into the night – down a steep hillside, and then over some terraced fields to a deep boulder-strewn ravine. It was here, after the sun had been up a few hours, that the master found all that the leopard had left of his servant. Incredible as it may seem, not one of the forty goats had received so much as a scratch.

I could go on and on, for there were many kills, and each one has its own tragic story, but I think I have said enough to convince you that the people of Garhwal had ample reason to be terrified of the man-eating leopard of Rudraprayag . . .

∗   ∗   ∗

It may be asked what the Government was doing all the years the Rudraprayag man-eater menaced the people of Garhwal. I hold no brief for the Government, but having spent ten weeks on the ground, during which time I walked many hundreds of miles and visited most of the villages in the affected area, I assert that the Government did everything in its power to remove the menace. Rewards were offered: the local population believed they amounted to ten thousand rupees in cash and the gift of two villages, sufficient inducement to make each one of the four thousand licensed gun-holders of Garhwal a prospective slayer of the man-eater. Picked *shikaris* were employed on liberal wages and were promised special rewards if their efforts were successful. More than three hundred special gun licenses over and above the four thousand in force were granted for the specific purpose of shooting the man-eater. Men of the Garhwal regiments stationed in Lansdowne were permitted to take their rifles with them when going home on leave, or were provided with sporting arms by their officers. Appeals were made through the press to sportsmen all over India to assist in the destruction of the leopard. Scores of traps of the drop-door type, with goats as bait, were erected on approaches to villages and on the roads frequented by the man-eater. Patwaris and other Government officials were supplied with poison for the purpose of poisoning human kills, and, last but not least, Government servants, often at great personal risk, spent all the time they could spare from their official duties in pursuit of the man-eater.

The total results from all these many and combined efforts were a slight gunshot wound which creased the pad of the leopard's left hind foot and shot away a small piece of skin from one of its toes, and an entry in Government records by the Deputy Commissioner of Garhwal that, so far from suffering any ill effects, the leopard appeared to thrive on, and be stimulated by, the poison he absorbed via human kills.

☆   ☆   ☆

It was during one of the intervals of Gilbert and Sullivan's *Yeomen of the Guard*, which was showing at the Chalet Theatre in Naini Tal in 1925, that I first had any definite news of the Rudraprayag man-eater.

I had heard casually that there was a man-eating leopard in Garhwal and had read articles in the press about the animal, but knowing that there were over four thousand licensed gun-holders in Garhwal, and a host of keen sportsmen in Lansdowne, only some seventy miles from Rudraprayag, I imagined that people were falling over each other in their eagerness to shoot the leopard and that a stranger under these circumstances would not be welcome.

It was with no little surprise therefore that, as I stood at the Chalet bar that night having a drink with a friend, I heard Michael Keene – then Chief Secretary to the Government of the United Provinces and later Governor of Assam – telling a group of men about the man-eater and trying to persuade them to go after it. His appeal, judging from the remark of one of the group, and endorsed by the others, was not received with any enthusiasm. The remark was, 'Go after a man-eater that has killed a hundred people? Not on your life!'

Next morning I paid Michael Keene a visit and got all the particulars I wanted. He was not able to tell me exactly where the man-eater was operating, and suggested my going to Rudraprayag and getting it touch with William Ibbotson. On my return home I found a letter from Ibbotson on my table.

Ibbotson – now Sir William Ibbotson and lately Adviser to the Governor of the United Provinces – had very recently been posted to Garhwal as Deputy Commissioner, and one of his first acts had been to try to rid his district of the man-eater. It was in this connection that he had written to me.

* * *

If you were to climb the hill to the east of Rudraprayag you would be able to see the greater portion of the five hundred square miles of country that the Rudraprayag man-eater ranged over. The area is divided into two more or less equal parts by the Alaknanda river, which, passing Karanprayag, flows south to Rudraprayag, where it is met by the Mandakini coming down from the north-west. The triangular bit of

country between the two rivers is less steep than the country along the
left bank of the Alaknanda, and there are consequently more villages in
the former area than in the latter.

From your elevated position, the cultivated land in the distance shows
up as a series of lines drawn across the face of the steep mountains. These
lines are terraced fields which vary in width from a yard to in some cases
fifty or more yards. The village buildings, you will note, are invariably set
at the upper end of the cultivated land; this is done with the object of
overlooking and protecting the cultivation from stray cattle and wild
animals, for except in very rare cases there are no hedges or fences
round the fields. The brown and green patches that make up most of the
landscape are, respectively, grassland and forests. Some of the villages,
you will observe, are entirely surrounded by grasslands, while others
are entirely surrounded by forests. The whole country, as you look down
on it, is rugged and rough, and is cut up by innumerable deep ravines
and rock cliffs. In this area there are only two roads, one starting from
Rudraprayag and going up to Kedarnath, and the other the main pilgrim
road to Badrinath. Both roads, up to the time I am writing about, were
narrow and rough and had never had a wheel of any kind on them.

It would be reasonable to assume that more human beings would be
killed in the villages surrounded by forests than in villages surrounded by
cultivated land. Had the man-eater been a tiger this would undoubtedly
have been the case, but to a man-eating leopard, which only operates
at night, the presence or absence of cover makes no difference, and the
only reason there were more kills in one village than another was due, in
the one case, to lack of precautions, and in the other, to the observance
of them.

The man-eater was an out-sized male leopard long past his prime, but
though he was old he was enormously strong. The ability of carnivora
to carry their kills to a place where they can feed undisturbed determines,
to a great extent, the place they choose to do their killing. To the
Rudraprayag man-eater all places were alike, for he was capable of

carrying the heaviest of his human victims for distances up to – on one occasion that I know of – four miles. On the occasion I refer to the leopard killed a fully grown man in his own house and carried his victim for two miles through dense scrub jungle. This was done for no apparent reason, for the kill had taken place in the early hours of the night and the leopard had not been followed up until noon of the next day.

Leopards – other than man-eaters – are the most easily killed of all animals in our jungles, for they have no sense of smell. More methods are employed in killing leopards than are employed in killing any other animal. These methods vary according to whether the leopard is being killed for sport, or for profit. The most exciting, and the most interesting, method of killing leopards for sport is to track them down in the jungles and, when they are located, stalk and shoot them. The easiest, and the most cruel method of killing leopards for profit is to insert a small and very highly explosive bomb in the flesh of an animal which has been killed by a leopard. Many villagers have learnt to make these bombs, and when one of them comes in contact with the leopard's teeth, it explodes and blows the leopard's jaws off. Death is instantaneous in some cases, but more often than not the unfortunate animal crawls away to die a lingering and very painful death, for the people who use the bombs have not the courage to follow the blood trail left by the leopard to dispatch it.

The tracking, locating and stalking of leopards, besides being exciting and interesting, is comparatively easy. For leopards have tender pads and keep to footpaths and game tracks as far as possible; they are not hard to locate, for practically every bird and animal in the jungle assists the hunter; and they are easy to stalk, for, though they are blessed with very keen sight and hearing, they are handicapped by having no sense of smell. The sportsman can therefore select the line of approach that best suits him, irrespective of the direction in which the wind is blowing.

Having tracked, located and stalked a leopard, far more pleasure is got from pressing the button of a camera than is ever got from pressing the trigger of a rifle. In the one case the leopard can be watched for hours, and there is no more graceful and interesting animal in the jungles to watch. The button of the camera can be pressed as fancy dictates to make a record which never loses its interest. In the other case a fleeting glimpse, one press of the trigger, and – if the aim has been true – the acquisition of a trophy which soon loses both its beauty and its interest.

*   *   *

No photographs or other means by which I could identify the man-eater by his pug-marks were available, so, until I had been given an opportunity of acquiring this information for myself, I decided to treat all leopards in the vicinity of Rudraprayag as suspect, and to shoot any that gave me the chance.

The day I arrived at Rudraprayag, I purchased two goats. One of these I tied up the following evening a mile along the pilgrim road; the other I took across the Alaknanda and tied up on a path running through some heavy scrub jungle where I found the old pug-marks of the big male leopard. On visiting the goats the following morning I found the one across the river had been killed and a small portion of it eaten. The goat had unquestionably been killed by a leopard, but had been eaten by a small animal, possibly a pine-marten.

Having received the news about the man-eater during the day, I decided to sit up over the goat, and at 3 p.m. took up my position in the branches of a small tree about fifty yards from the kill. During the three hours I sat in the tree I had no indication, from either animals or birds, that the leopard was anywhere in the vicinity, and as dusk was falling I slipped off the tree, cut the cord tethering the goat – which the leopard had made no attempt to break the previous night – and set off for the bungalow.

I have already admitted that I had very little previous experience of man-eating leopards, but I had met a few man-eating tigers, and from the time I left the tree until I reached the bungalow I took every precaution to guard against a sudden attack; and it was fortunate that I did so.

I made an early start next morning, and near the gate of the bungalow I picked up the tracks of a big male leopard. These tracks I followed back to a densely wooded ravine which crossed the path close to where the goat was lying. The goat had not been touched during the night.

The leopard that had followed me could only have been the man-eater, and for the rest of the day I walked as many miles as my legs would carry me, telling all the people in the villages I visited, and all whom I met on the roads, that the man-eater was on our side of the river, and warning them to be careful.

Nothing happened that day, but the next day, just as I was finishing breakfast after a long morning prospecting the jungles beyond Golabrai, a very agitated man dashed into the bungalow to tell me that a woman had been killed by the man-eater the previous night in a village on the hill above the bungalow – the same hill and almost the exact spot from where you obtained your bird's-eye view of the five hundred square miles of country the man-eater was operating over.

Within a few minutes I collected all the things I needed – a spare rifle and a shotgun, cartridges, rope, and a length of fishing line – and set off up the steep hill accompanied by the villager and two of my men. It was a sultry day, and though the distance was not great – three miles at the most – the climb of four thousand feet in the hot sun was very trying and I arrived at the village in a bath of sweat.

The story of the husband of the woman who had been killed was soon told. After their evening meal, which had been eaten by the light of the fire, the woman collected the metal pots and pans that had been used and carried them to the door to wash, while the man sat down to have a smoke. On reaching the door the woman sat down on the doorstep and as she did so the utensils clattered to the ground. There was not sufficient light for the man to see what happened, and when he received no answer to his urgent call he rushed forward and shut and barred the door. 'Of what use,' he said, 'would it have been to risk my life in trying to recover a dead body?' His logic was sound, though heartless; and I gathered that the grief he showed was occasioned not so much by the loss of his wife, as by the loss of that son and heir whom he had expected to see born within the next few days.

The door, where the woman had been seized, opened on to a four-foot-wide lane that ran for fifty yards between two rows of houses. On hearing the clatter of the falling pots and pans, followed by the urgent call of the man to his wife, every door in the lane had been instantaneously shut. The marks on the ground showed that the leopard had dragged the unfortunate woman the length of the lane, then killed her, and carried her down the lane for a hundred yards into a small ravine that bordered some terraced fields. Here he ate his meal, and here he left the pitiful remains.

The body lay in the ravine at one end of the narrow terraced field, at the other end of which, forty yards away, was a leafless and stunted walnut tree in whose branches a hayrick had been built, four feet from the ground and six feet tall. In this hayrick I decided to sit.

Starting from near the body, a narrow path ran into the ravine. On this path were the pug-marks of the leopard that had killed the woman, and they were identical with the pug-marks of the leopard that had followed me two nights previously from the killed goat to the Rudra-prayag bungalow. The pug-marks were of an out-sized male leopard long past its prime, with a slight defect where the bullet fired four years previously had creased the pad of his left hind paw.

I procured two stout eight-foot bamboos from the village and drove them into the ground close to the perpendicular bank that divided the field where the body was lying from the field below. To these bamboos I fixed my spare rifle and shotgun securely, tied lengths of dressed silk fishing-line to the triggers, looped the lines back over the trigger-guards, and fastened them to two stakes driven into the hillside on the far side of, a little above, the path. If the leopard came along the path he had used the previous night there was a reasonable chance of his pulling on the lines and shooting himself; on the other hand, if he avoided them, or came by any other way, and I fired at him while he was on the kill, he would be almost certain to run into the trap which lay on his most natural line of retreat. Both the leopard, because of its protective colouring, and the body, which had been stripped of all clothing, would be invisible in the dark; so to give me an idea of the direction in which to fire, I took a slab of white rock from the ravine and put it on the edge of the field, about a foot from the near side of the body.

The sun was near setting, and the view of the Ganges valley, with the snowy Himalayas in the background showing bluish pink under the level rays of the setting sun, was a feast for the eyes. Almost before I realised it, daylight had faded out of the sky and the night had come.

Darkness, when used in connection with night, is a relative term and has no fixed standard; what to one man would be pitch dark, to another would be dark, and to a third moderately dark. To me, having spent so much of my life in the open, the night is never dark, unless the sky is overcast with heavy clouds. I do not wish to imply that I can see as well by night as by day; but I can see quite well enough to find my way through any jungle or, for that matter, over any ground. I had placed the white stone near the body only as a precaution, for I had hoped that the starlight, with the added reflection from the snowy range, would give me sufficient light to shoot by.

But my luck was out; for night had hardly fallen when there was a flash of lightning, followed by distant thunder, and in a few minutes the sky was heavily overcast. Just as the first big drops of a deluge began to fall, I heard a stone roll into the ravine, and a minute later the loose straw on the ground below me was being scratched up. The leopard had arrived; and while I sat in torrential rain with the icy-cold wind whistling through my wet clothes, he lay dry and snug in the straw below. The storm was one of the worst I have ever experienced, and while it was at its height, I saw a lantern being carried towards the village, and marvelled at the

THE MAN-EATING LEOPARD OF RUDRAPRAYAG

courage of the man who carried it. It was not until some hours later that I learnt that the man who so gallantly braved both the leopard and the storm had done a forced march of over thirty miles from Pauri to bring me the electric night-shooting light the Government had promised me; the arrival of the light three short hours earlier might . . . but regrets are vain, and who can say that the fourteen people who died later would have had a longer span of life if the leopard had not buried its teeth in their throats? And again, even if the light had arrived in time there is no certainty that I should have killed the leopard that night.

*   *   *

A guide was waiting for us at the bridge, and he took us up a very steep ridge and along a grassy hillside, and then down into a deep and densely wooded ravine with a small stream flowing through it. Here we found the patwari and some twenty men guarding the kill.

The kill was a very robust and fair girl, some eighteen or twenty years of age. She was lying on her face with her hands by her sides. Every vestige of clothing had been stripped from her, and she had been licked by the leopard from the soles of her feet to her neck, in which were four great teeth-marks; only a few pounds of flesh had been eaten from the upper portion of her body, and a few pounds from the lower portion.

The drums we had heard as we came up the hill were being beaten by the men who were guarding the kill, and as it was then about 2 pm and there was no chance of the leopard being anywhere in the vicinity, we went up to the village to brew ourselves some tea, taking the patwari and the guard with us.

After tea we went and had a look at the house where the girl had been killed. It was a stone-built house, consisting of one room, situated in the midst of terraced fields some two or three acres in extent, and it was occupied by the girl, her husband, and their six-month child.

Two days previous to the kill, the husband had gone to Pauri to give evidence in a land dispute case, and had left his father in charge of the house. On the night of the kill, after the girl and her father-in-law had partaken of their evening meal and it was getting near time to retire for the night, the girl, who had been nursing her child, handed it over to her father-in-law, unlatched the door, and stepped outside to squat down – I have already mentioned that there are no sanitary conveniences in the houses of our hill-folk.

When the child was transferred from the mother to the grandfather, it started crying, so even if there had been any sound from outside – and I am sure there was none – he would not have heard it. It was a dark night. After waiting for a few minutes the man called to the girl; and receiving no answer he called again. Then he got up and hurriedly closed and latched the door.

Rain had fallen in the evening and it was easy to reconstruct the scene. Shortly after the rain had stopped, the leopard, coming from the direction of the village, had crouched down behind a rock in the field, about thirty yards to the left front of the door. Here it had lain for some time – possibly listening to the man and the girl talking. When the girl opened the door she squatted down on the right-hand side, partly turning her back on the leopard, who had crept round the far side of the rock, covered the twenty yards separating him from the corner of the house with belly to ground and, creeping along close to the wall of the house, had caught the girl from behind, and dragged her to the rock. Here, when the girl was dead, or possibly when the man called out in alarm, the leopard had picked her up and, holding her high, so that no mark of hand or foot showed on the soft newly ploughed ground, had carried her across one field, down a three-foot bank, and across another field which ended up in a twelve-foot drop on to a well-used footpath. Down this drop the leopard had sprung with the girl – who weighed about eleven stone – in his mouth, and some idea of his strength will be realised from the fact that when he landed on the footpath he did not let any portion of her body come into contact with the ground.

Crossing the footpath he had gone straight down the hill for half a mile, to the spot where he had undressed the girl. After eating a little of her, he had left her lying in a little glade of emerald-green grass, under the shade of a tree roofed over with dense creepers.

At about four o'clock we went down to sit over the kill, taking the petrol-lamp and the night-shooting light with us.

It was reasonable to assume that the leopard had heard the noise the villagers made when searching for the girl, and later when guarding the body, and if it returned to the kill it would do so with great caution; so we decided not to sit near the kill, and select a tree about sixty yards away on the hill overlooking the glade.

This tree, a stunted oak, was growing out of the hill at almost a right angle, and after we had hidden the petrol-lamp in a little hollow and covered it over with pine-needles, Ibbotson took his seat in the fork of a tree from where he had a clear view of the kill, while I sat on the trunk with my back facing him and facing the hill; Ibbotson was to take the shot, while I saw to our safety. As the shooting light was not functioning – possibly because the battery had faded out – our plan was to sit up as long as Ibbotson could see to shoot and then, with the help of the petrol-lamp, get back to the village where we hoped to find that our men had arrived from Rudraprayag.

We had not the time to prospect the ground, but the villagers had informed us that there was heavy jungle to the east of the kill, to which they felt sure the leopard had retired when they drove it off. If the leopard came from this direction, Ibbotson would see it long before it got to the glade and would get an easy shot, for his rifle was fitted with a telescopic sight which not only made for accurate shooting, but which also gave us an extra half-hour, as we had found from tests. When a minute of daylight more or less made the difference between success and failure, this modification of the light factor is very important.

The sun was setting behind the high hills to the west, and we had been in shadow for some minutes when a kakar dashed down the hill, barking, from the direction in which we had been told there was heavy jungle. On the shoulder of the hill the animal pulled up, and after barking in one spot went away on the far side and the sound died away in the distance.

The kakar had undoubtedly been alarmed by a leopard, and though it was quite possible that there were other leopards in that area, my hopes had been raised, and when I looked round at Ibbotson I saw that he too was keyed up, and that he had both hands on his rifle.

Light was beginning to fade, but was good enough to shoot by even without the aid of the telescopic sight, when a pine-cone dislodged from behind some low bushes thirty yards above us came rolling down the hill and struck the tree close to my feet. The leopard had arrived and, possibly suspecting danger, had taken a line that would allow him to prospect from a safe place on the hill all the ground in the vicinity of his kill. Unfortunately, in so doing he had got our tree in a direct line with the kill, and though I, who was showing no outline, might escape observation, he would be certain to see Ibbotson, who was sitting in the fork of the tree.

When sufficient light for me to shoot by had long since gone, and Ibbotson's telescopic sight was no longer of any use to him, we heard the leopard coming stealthily down towards the tree. It was then time to take action, so I asked Ibbotson to take my place, while I retrieved the lamp. This lamp was of German make, and was called a petromax. It gave a brilliant light but, with its long body and longer handle, was not designed to be used as a lantern in the jungle.

I am a little taller than Ibbotson, and suggested that I should carry the lamp, but Ibbotson said that he could manage all right, and, moreover, that he would rather depend on my rifle than his own. So we set off, Ibbotson leading and I following with both hands on my rifle.

Fifty yards from the tree, while climbing over a rock, Ibbotson slipped, the base of the lamp came into violent contact with the rock, and the mantle fell in dust to the bottom of the lamp. The streak of blue flame directed from the nozzle on to the petrol reservoir gave sufficient light for us to see where to put our feet, but the question was how long we should have even this much light. Ibbotson was of the opinion that he could carry the lamp for three minutes before it burst. Three minutes, in which to do a stiff climb of half a mile, over ground on which it was necessary to change direction every few steps to avoid huge rocks and thornbushes, and possibly followed – and actually followed as we found later – by a man-eater, was a terrifying prospect.

There are events in one's life which, no matter how remote, never fade from memory; the climb up the hill in the dark was for me one of them. When we eventually reached the footpath our troubles were not ended, for the path was a series of buffalo wallows, and we did not know where our men were. Alternatively slipping on wet ground and stumbling over unseen rocks, we at last came to some stone steps which took off from the path and went up to the right. Climbing these steps we found a small courtyard, on the far side of which was a door. We heard the gurgling of a hookah as we came up the steps, so I kicked the door and shouted to the inmates to open. As no answer came, I took out a box of matches and shook it, crying that if the door was not open in a minute I would set the thatch alight. On this an agitated voice came from inside the house, begging me not to set the house on fire, and saying that the door was being opened – a minute later, first the inner door and then the outer door were opened, and in two strides Ibbotson and I were in the house, slamming the inner door, and putting our backs to it.

☆　☆　☆

Ibbotson returned from Pauri on the last day of March, and the following morning, while we were having breakfast, we received a report that a leopard had called very persistently the previous night near a village to the north-west of Rudraprayag.

Half a mile to the north of the village, on the shoulder of the great mountain, there was a considerable area of rough and broken ground where there were enormous rocks and caves, and deep holes in which the locals said their forefathers had quarried copper. Over the whole of this area there was scrub jungle, heavy in some places and light in others, extending down the hillside to within half a mile of the terraced fields above the village.

I had long suspected that the man-eater used this ground as a hideout when he was in the vicinity of Rudraprayag, and I had frequently climbed to a commanding position above the broken ground in the hope of finding him basking on the rocks in the early morning sun, for leopards are very fond of doing this in a cold climate, and it is a very common way of shooting them, for all that is needed is a little patience, and accuracy of aim.

After an early lunch Ibbotson and I set out armed with our .275 rifles, and accompanied by one of Ibbotson's men carrying a short length of rope. At the village we purchased a young male goat – the leopard having killed all the goats I had purchased from time to time.

From the village, a rough goat track ran straight up the hill to the edge of the broken ground, where it turned left, and after running across the face of the hill for a hundred yards carried on round the shoulder of the mountain. The track where it ran across the hill was bordered on the upper side by scattered bushes, and on the steep lower side by short grass.

Having tied the goat to a peg firmly driven into the ground at the bend in the track, about ten yards below the scrub jungle, we went down the hill for a hundred and fifty yards to where there were some big rocks, behind which we concealed ourselves. The goat was one of the best callers I have ever heard, and while its shrill and piercing bleat continued there was no necessity for us to watch him, for he had been very securely tied and there was no possibility of the leopard carrying him away.

The sun – a fiery red ball – was a hand's breadth from the snow mountains above Kedarnath when we took up our position behind the rocks, and half an hour later, when we had been in shadow for a few minutes, the goat suddenly stopped calling. Creeping to the side of the rock and looking through a screen of grass, I saw the goat with ears cocked, looking up towards the bushes; as I watched, the goat shook his head, and backed to the full length of the rope.

The leopard had undoubtedly come, attracted by the calling of the goat, and that he had not pounced before the goat became aware of his presence was proof that he was suspicious. Ibbotson's aim would be more accurate than mine, for his rifle was fitted with a telescopic sight, so I made room for him, and as he laid down and raised his rifle I whispered to him to examine carefully the bushes in the direction in which the goat was looking, for I felt sure that if the goat could see the leopard – and all the indications were that it could – Ibbotson should also be able to see it through his powerful telescope. For minutes Ibbotson kept his eye to the telescope and then shook his head, laid down the rifle, and made room for me.

The goat was standing in exactly the same position in which I had last seen it, and taking direction from it I fixed the telescope on the same bush at which he was looking. The flicker of an eyelid, or the very least movement of ear or even whiskers, would have been visible through the telescope, but though I watched for minutes I too could see nothing.

When I took my eye away from the telescope I noted that the light was rapidly fading, and that the goat now showed as a red and white blur on the hillside. We had a long way to go and waiting longer would be both useless and dangerous, so getting to my feet I told Ibbotson it was time for us to make a move.

Going up to the goat – who from the time he had stopped bleating had not made a sound – we freed it from the peg, and with the man leading it we set off for the village. The goat quite evidently had never had a rope round its neck before and objected violently to being led, so I told the man to take the rope off – my experience being that when a goat is freed after having been tied up in the jungle, through fear or for want of companionship it follows at heel like a dog. This goat, however, had ideas of its own, and no sooner had the man removed the rope from its neck, that it turned and ran up the track.

It was too good a calling goat to abandon – it had attracted the leopard once, and might do so again. Moreover, we had only a few hours previously paid good money for it, so we in turn ran up the track in hot pursuit. At the bend, the goat turned to the left, and we lost sight of it. Keeping to the track, as the goat had done, we went to the shoulder of the hill where a considerable extent of the hill, clothed in short grass, was visible, and as the goat was nowhere in sight we decided it had taken a short cut back to the village, and started to retrace our steps. I was leading, and as we got half-way along the hundred yards of track, bordered on the upper side by scattered bushes and on the steep lower side by short grass, I saw something white on the track in front of me. The light had nearly gone, and on cautiously approaching the white object I found it was the goat – laid head and tail on the narrow track, in the only position in which it could have been laid to prevent it from rolling down the steep hillside. Blood was oozing from its throat, and when I placed my hand on it the muscles were still twitching.

It was as though the man-eater – for no other leopard would have killed the goat and laid it on the track – had said "Here, if you want your goat so badly, take it; and as it is now dark, and you have a long way to go, we will see which of you lives to reach the village."

*   *   *

It was not long after this occurrence the dogs were unmistakably barking at a leopard, which quite possibly had seen the man with the lantern and was now coming down the road on its way to the shelter.

At first the dogs barked in the direction of the road, but after a little while they turned and barked in my direction. The leopard had now quite evidently caught sight of the sleeping goat and lain down out of sight of the dogs – which had stopped barking – to consider his next move. I knew that the leopard had arrived, and I also knew he was using my tree to stalk the goat, and the question that was tormenting me as the long moments dragged by was whether he would skirt around the goat and kill one of the pilgrims, or whether he would kill the goat and give me a shot.

During all the nights I had sat in the tree I adopted a position that would enable me to discharge my rifle with the minimum of movement and in the minimum of time. The distance between the goat and my machan was about twenty feet, but the night was so dark under the dense foliage of the tree that my straining eyes could not penetrate even this short distance, so I closed them and concentrated on my hearing.

My rifle, to which I had a small electric torch attached, was pointing in the direction of the goat, and I was just beginning to think that the leopard – assuming it was the man-eater – had reached the shelter and was selecting a human victim, when there was a rush from the foot of the tree, and the goat's bell tinkled sharply. Pressing the button of the torch I saw that the sights of the rifle were aligned on the shoulder of a leopard, and without having to move the rifle a fraction of an inch I pressed the trigger, and as I did so the torch went out.

Torches in those days were not in as general use as they are now, and mine was the first I had ever possessed. I had carried it for several months and never had occasion to use it, and I did not know the life of the battery, or that it was necessary to test it. When I pressed the button on this occasion the torch only gave one dim flash and then went out, and I was again in darkness without knowing what the result of my shot had been.

The echo of my shot was dying away in the valley when the pundit opened his door and called out to ask if I needed any help. I was at the time listening with all my ears for any sounds that might come from the leopard, so I did not answer him, and he hurriedly shut the door.

The leopard had been lying across the road with his head away from me when I fired, and I was vaguely aware of his having sprung over the goat and gone down the hillside, and just before the pundit had called I thought I heard what may have been a gurgling sound, but of this I could not be sure. The pilgrims had been aroused by my shot but, after murmuring for a few minutes, they resumed their sleep. The goat appeared to be unhurt, for from the sound of the bell I could tell that he was moving about and apparently eating the grass of which he was given a liberal supply each night.

I had fired my shot at 10pm. As the moon was not due to rise for several hours, and as there was nothing I could do in the meantime, I made myself comfortable, and listened and smoked.

Hours later the moon lit up the crest of the hills on the far side of the Ganges and slowly crept down into the valley, and a little later I saw it rise over the top of the hill behind me. As soon as it was overhead I climbed to the top of the tree, but found that the spreading branches impeded my view. Descending again to the machan, I climbed out on the branches spreading over the road, but from here also I found it was not possible to see down the hillside in the direction in which I thought the leopard had gone. It was then 3am, and two hours later the moon began to pale. When nearby objects became visible in the light of the day that was being born in the east, I descended from the tree and was greeted by a friendly bleat from the goat.

Beyond the goat, and at the very edge of the road, there was a long low rock, and on this rock there was an inch-wide streak of blood; the leopard from which the blood had come could only have lived a minute or two, so dispensing with the precautions usually taken when following up the blood trail of carnivores, I scrambled down off the road and, taking up the trail on the far side of the rock, followed it for fifty yards, to where the leopard was lying dead. He had slid backwards into a hole in the ground, in which he was lying not crouched up, but with his chin resting on the edge of the hole.

No marks by which I could identify the dead animal were visible, even so I never for one moment doubted that the leopard in the hole was the man-eater. But here was no fiend, who while watching me through the long night hours had rocked and rolled with silent fiendish laughter at my vain attempts to outwit him, and licked his lips in anticipation of the time when, finding me off my guard for one brief moment, he would get the opportunity he was waiting for of burying his teeth in my throat. Here was only an old leopard, who differed from others of his kind in that his muzzle was grey and his lips lacked whiskers; the best hated and most feared animal in all India, whose only crime – not against the laws of nature, but against the laws of man – was that he had shed human blood, with no object of terrorising man, but only in order that he might live; and who now, with his chin resting on the rim of the hole and his eyes half-closed, was peacefully sleeping his long last sleep.

✳   ✳   ✳

I have on other occasions witnessed gratitude, but never as I witnessed it that day at Rudraprayag, first at the Inspection Bungalow and later at a reception in the bazaar.

"He killed our only son, sahib, and we being old, our house is now desolate."

"He ate the mother of my five children, and the youngest is but a few months old, and there is none in the home now to care for the children, or to cook the food."

"My son was taken ill at night and no one dared to go to the hospital for medicine, and so he died."

Tragedy upon pitiful tragedy, and while I listened, the ground around my feet was strewn with flowers.

CHAPTER 4

Leopards in Ceylon

SIR SAMUEL W. BAKER

Although born in London, the son of a wealthy West India merchant, the restless Samuel Baker travelled to the island of Ceylon where he founded an agricultural settlement at Nuwara Eliya, a mountain health resort. Aided by his brother he brought emigrants from England, together with choice breeds of cattle, and before long the settlement was a success. While in Ceylon he published, as a result of many adventurous hunting expeditions, "The Rifle and Hound in Ceylon" (1853), and two years later "Eight Years' Wanderings in Ceylon" (1855), from which this chapter is reprinted. In March 1861 he started his first exploration in central Africa. Three years later he discovered Lake Albert which later was proved to be one of the two great reservoirs of the Nile – the other being Lake Victoria.

The leopard varies from eight to nine feet in length, and has been known to reach even ten feet. His body is covered with black 'rings', with a rich brown centre – his muzzle and legs are speckled with black 'spots', and his weight is from 110 to 170 pounds. There is little or no distinction between the leopard and the panther, they are synonymous terms for a variety of species in different countries.

The power of the animal is wonderful in proportion to its weight. I have seen a full-grown bullock with its neck broken by a leopard. It is the popular belief that the effect is produced by a blow of the paw; it is not simply the blow, but it is the combination of the weight, the muscular power, and the momentum of the spring, which renders the effects of a leopard's attack so surprising.

Few leopards rush boldly upon their prey like a dog; they stalk their game, and advance crouchingly, making use of every object that will afford them cover until they are within a few bounds of their victim. Then the immense power of muscle is displayed in the concentrated energy of the spring; he flies through the air and settles on the throat, usually throwing his own body over the animal, while his teeth and claws are fixed on the neck. This is the manner in which the spine of an animal is broken, by a sudden twist, and not simply by a blow.

The blow from the paw is nevertheless immensely powerful, and at one stroke will rip open a bullock like a knife; but the after effects of the wound are still more to be dreaded than the force of the stroke. There is a peculiar poison in the mouth, which is highly dangerous. This is caused by the putrid flesh which they are constantly tearing, and which is apt to cause gangrene by inoculation.

It is a prevalent idea that a leopard will not eat putrid meat, but that he forsakes a rotten carcass and seeks fresh prey. There is no doubt that a natural love of slaughter induces him to a constant search for prey, but it has nothing to do with the daintiness of his appetite. A leopard will eat any stinking offal that offers, and I once had a melancholy proof of this.

I was returning from a morning's hunting; it was a bitter day, the rain was pouring in torrents, the wind was blowing a gale, and sweeping the water in sheets along the earth. The hounds were following at my horse's heels, with their ears and sterns down, looking very miserable, and altogether it was a day when man and beast should have been at home. Presently upon turning a corner of the road, I saw a Malabar boy of about sixteen years of age, squatted shivering by the road-side. His only covering being a scanty cloth round his loins, I told him to get up, and go on, or he would be starved with cold. He said something in reply, which I could not understand, and, rejecting my first warning, I rode on. It was only two miles to my house, but upon arrival I could not help thinking that the boy must be ill, and having watched the gate for some time, to see if he passed by, I determined to send for him.

Accordingly I started off a couple of men with order to carry him up if he were sick.

They returned in little more than an hour, but the poor boy was dead! Sitting crouched in the same position in which I had seen him. He must have died of cold and starvation; he was a mere skeleton.

I sent men to the spot and had him buried by the road-side, and a few days after I rode down to see where they had laid him.

A quantity of fresh-turned earth lay scattered about, mingled with fragments of rags. Bones much gnawed lay here and there on the road, and a putrid skull had rolled from a shapeless hole among a confused and horrible heap. The leopards had scratched him up and then devoured him; their footprints were still fresh upon the damp ground.

CHAPTER 5

The Kantali Leopard

HENRY STOREY, 1900

One of my favourite books about Old Ceylon is Ceylon Beaten Track *by my old headmaster at St Thomas Preparatory School in Colombo – W. T. Keble. This book was first published in 1940. In his book, which I generally carry around with me whenever I travel in Sri Lanka, Keble recounts a story told by the renowned Ceylon sportsman Harry Storey in 1900. In Kantalai village he was reminded of the now famous leopard story, which I reproduce exactly as Harry Storey related it. There have been many gruesome leopard stories; however the following is remarkable in that it is one of the few examples of a human surviving an attack by a leopard.*

"I was sitting on a small ant-hill a little way out in the open in an angle of the Park, with jungle on either hand and behind me, and I presently saw a small animal walking through the grass, about 50 yards ahead, across my front from left to right. I saw it was a feline of some sort, but could only see its head and the top of its back above the grass, which was here about 18 inches high. It struck me at once that it might be that seldom-seen animal *felis viverrina*, the fishing cat, so I cocked my rifle, a single-barrelled breech-loading .303 be it noted, and fired at it when it was just opposite me. I missed, the bullet striking the ground just under its nose, and the little animal turned and bounded back to the jungle, whereupon the old Kapurala came up to me and asked what I had shot at. I said I thought it was one of the big wild cats, but he said it looked suspiciously like a leopard cub.

"We walked towards the jungle into which it had disappeared, and I halted about fifteen yards from it, whilst the old man began to look for 'sign'. I was standing at my ease with my rifle uncocked, thrown across my left arm, thinking of nothing in particular, when suddenly the old man, without a word, turned and ran like a madman past me towards the open park, his eyes bulging out with terror. I gazed at him, uncomprehending, in surprise, when glancing towards the forest I saw a full-grown, but small and thickset, leopard emerge from the jungle like a flash. It passed me at about five yards, perfectly silent, going not in leaps and bounds but belly to the ground like a greyhound, and catching up to the old man, sprang on to his back, the impetus knocking the man down, so that both rolled head over heels.

"The leopard landed fair on the man's back and shoulders, its fore-paws catching him round the neck, and its head, with its murderous jaws wide open, actually lay on top of the man's head like a hideous cap. The shock knocked the old man down, and he rolled head over heels beyond him. By this time, of course, I had my rifle ready, as I expected the brute, on rising, would go for the old man and thus give me a chance of a shot. However it did nothing of the sort. It recovered its feet in an instant and launched itself at me, all in one movement, so to speak, without any pause, and with such fearful rapidity that, prepared as I was, I had only just enough time to throw my rifle to my shoulder and pull the trigger without seeing a sight or anything – a regular snapshot.

"If I never saw 'battle, murder, and sudden death' before, I saw it coming towards me then in awful silence, mouth wide open, showing some very powerful teeth, ears laid back, and eyes fixed on me with a baneful glare; but at my shot the flying figure collapsed and came rolling over and over to my very feet. As quick as thought I dropped my rifle, and pulling out my hunting-knife, a big heavy one with a double-edged blade, plunged it into the back behind the shoulder.

"Well and good if I had stabbed and withdrawn the knife very quickly; but I did not. Like an ass, I wrenched it about in the wound a bit, with the result of galvanising the leopard into comparatively active life, for it turned suddenly over, knocked the knife flying out of my hand, grabbed me by the left leg with its forepaws, and pulled me down on top of it. I rolled over to one side at once, desperately pulled at its paws with my right hand and kicked as desperately at it with my right foot, whilst my left hand was occupied fending its horrible head away from my face, as we lay side by side, for it was struggling hard to get its teeth into me. Trying to get it by the throat, my left hand unfortunately got into its mouth, and it promptly took hold hot and strong. So I had to leave it at that, but thrust its head away to the full stretch of my arm and then got to work pulling its claws out of me.

"This I succeeded in doing after a while, and by a desperate wrench getting my left hand free, rolled rapidly over; but I was not quick enough, for out came a paw, got me by the thigh, and hauled me back again. More kicking and struggling, and again I got free, but again that awful paw hauled me back like a bundle of old clothes. Another desperate effort and I managed to roll out of reach, got up, staggered to my rifle, reloaded and shot the brute dead; and then, as the whole universe seemed to be going round and round in a variety of colours, I dropped to the ground to consider matters a bit, feeling deathly sick. However, it was getting late, so I soon arose and began to inspect the damages. I perceived my left trouser leg to be dyed brilliant scarlet, as was my shoe, and, on pulling up the trousers, two of the various tears and holes in my leg spouted blood out about a foot, which sight fairly startled me. I yelled to the old man to get me a stick, but he seemed too dazed, so I twisted my handkerchief round my leg as tight as I could without the help of a stick, and then got up to have a look at the old man. He was torn a bit down the back, round the neck, and one claw had penetrated very close

to the throat. I wrapped one of his cloths around his neck to stop the streaming blood, and we turned towards camp, a terrible two miles away. My wounds got very painful and stiff, and my left hand was about useless; but we struggled on, getting to camp whilst there was still light enough to see our way.

"Next day I sent off our only other tracker to his village ten miles away for bearers, and they, arriving in the afternoon, made a sort of stretcher for me out of jungle sticks, on which the next day they carried me fifteen miles to the Kantali Rest House.

"I had about a month in bed, but eventually recovered all right with no ill effects, and I am glad to be able to say the old man also recovered, and has often been out with me since."

CHAPTER 6

The Man-Eater of Punanai

CHRISTOPHER ONDAATJE

At noon on 22 May 1924, Captain R. Shelton Agar received a telegram from the Government Agent, Eastern Province, Ceylon. "Reward Rs. 100/– offered destruction man-eating leopard Punanai ten miles from Valachenai ferry," it stated. Captain Agar hardly needed one hundred rupees. He was a prosperous estate owner and tea planter in the Hatton district, with long family connections to the colony. But the offer made him "quite excited", as he wrote later, because he had never heard of such a leopard before. He had shot leopard at a water-hole, he had watched a leopard kill, he had stumbled upon leopards in the jungle, he had killed rogue elephants and other mad beasts, but the idea of going after a clever cat with a taste for human flesh struck him as an "interesting undertaking".

In 1989 I wrote a book, a factual book, which had at its heart only half the truth. Perhaps that's not so unusual; many a non-fiction writer has embellished or exaggerated, slightly shifted time or place, fleshed out bystanders into centre stage characters, all to increase the evocative charge of the narrative. But in the case of *The Man-Eater of Punanai* the opposite was true. It was not that my experiences needed spice – a pinch of creative fabrication to season the humdrum reality of my return to Sri Lanka. Far from it.

The book was to be a story of exploration and discovery, partly into my own family history, but also into the notorious man-eater of Punanai, a leopard that wreaked havoc, destroying many lives in a small village in old Ceylon in the 1920s. I travelled through Sri Lanka, returning to familiar haunts that I had not seen since I was a boy, trying to comprehend what had driven my father's self-destruction, taking careful, often frightened steps through a land so much changed since my childhood and now in the grip of civil war.

Each evening I updated my journal as fully and accurately as possible, doing my best to capture the sights and sounds and smells of the place, knowing these notes would form the basis of my book, aware of how quickly the sensory memory fades. My last stop was Punanai itself, an extremely dangerous place to visit at the end of the 1980s. Nevertheless, I was determined to see for myself the scene of the leopard's crimes and ultimate death.

On my return to England I spent long hours working on my travel journal in relative safety, interweaving autobiography, family history and research until a manuscript finally took shape. This was my first book on Ceylon and most personal book to date, the symbol of the start of a new life free from the constraints and obligations of the North American business world. It had been a bittersweet journey into my own past and I had forced myself to address occasionally painful feelings about my own childhood in Ceylon. Here on paper was my struggle to understand my father, and here too a record of the astonishing events in Punanai, both in 1924 and 1989. I was excited and more than a little nervous about how my editors might receive it. The answer was not what I would ever have expected.

They were pleased enough. With a few tweaks and revisions (and with my photographs included) it could make a decent book. But there was one major problem: my account of the trip to Punanai. The editors simply refused to believe it. They claimed it was just too far-fetched and their worry was that, even if readers could credit that the old man in

Punanai was there, they wouldn't believe that anyone could survive such a leopard attack.

The story of the man-eater was bound up with my childhood and my father. I first heard it on that day we spent together in Yala National Park in 1946, when I saw my first leopard. My father was at his best that day. He saw my enthusiasm for the leopard – an animal whose elusive beauty caught my attention more than any other – even then. I have often wondered what so drew me and held me all these years. Many of the big cats share the leopard's grace and majesty, but none has such an air of mystery and of evil.

My father, however, was less concerned with the exact cause of my excitement, only prompted to encourage it. He answered my many questions as best he could, but couldn't supply the facts and figures I needed. So in the evening I turned to our trackers and asked them to tell me everything they knew. 'Do they eat people?' I asked, and that was how I first heard the story of the man-eater of Punanai. It was also one of my first experiences of the Sinhala talent for storytelling. Despite being told in pidgin English – or perhaps because of it – the story was gripping and the trackers spared no horrifying detail, no colourful gory description, in bringing it to life.

Over the course of a year or two in the early 1920s, an exceptionally dangerous and audacious leopard had killed and devoured at least twenty human beings in the region of Punanai, keeping the tiny village in terror. Villagers disappeared from their mud huts in the night. Coolies vanished as they worked on the railway lines. Bearers walking empty stretches of the road to Batticaloa were ambushed and eaten. Children were stolen in broad daylight . . . The state of panic persisted until an English tea planter and sportsman, Captain Shelton Agar, finally shot the beast in 1924.

I was at the time an impressionable twelve-year-old and the story frightened me out of my wits. Yala in the South East, where we were travelling, was very wild then and I thought Punanai might be close by. The bungalow where we were staying was remote and dangerously exposed. There was only the light of the kerosene lamps, and I had a vivid imagination. Not that it took much imagination, as I lay on a cot on the verandah in the hot night, to fear a leopard moving in the dark jungle just beyond the parapet.

The story came back to me when I was thinking about returning to Sri Lanka. Perhaps it was only natural that my efforts to recapture my past should lead to this childhood tale coming back to haunt me. I decided that I would face my memories of my father and the story of the man-eater together. I would revisit Yala and Punanai and spend time rediscovering my own Old World that had changed so much.

This journey eventually became *The Man-Eater of Punanai*. It marked my steps away from my old life and my reconciliation with the past, interweaving family history, autobiography and my rediscovery of Ceylon by following the man-eater. I also tried to reflect on the civil war that was raging in Sri Lanka. The conflict between the Tamil Tigers and the Sinhalese had been ongoing since the early 1970s, but by 1988 the situation had become significantly more complicated. Conflict between rival Tamil factions sprung up in the north, while Sinhalese factions such as the anarchist JVP were active in the south. Meanwhile both the Tigers and the Sri Lankan government wanted to oust the 60,000 Indian peace-keeping troops. This was the violent confusion into which I walked. There were warnings everywhere about the dangers of doing this or that, going here or there, and my journey to Punanai became a deadly safari into the heartland of the Tamil Tigers.

★   ★   ★

At the end of a long, emotionally draining journey fraught with dangers, entering Punanai was the final risk. The road lay through guerrilla-infested jungle; the Tigers were in control of the area after taking it from the Indian troops and were keeping it from the Sri Lankan army. Neither the Tigers nor the Sri Lankan army were keen to allow strangers into the area. My guide, Mahinda Rajapakse ('Raja'), was worried for my safety, but refused to let me go by myself. Although Sinhalese, he had dark skin and spoke Tamil fluently. He warned, however, that I could be mistaken for a foreign correspondent and the threat of ambush was real. I must not appear to be too eager for information or photographs.

We drove in silence through arid scrub and tall grass – ideal ambush country for leopards or for men. But we saw nobody until just to the west of Punanai when two armed soldiers waved us down at an LTTE[1] checkpoint. They took Raja into a hut for questioning. Where were we going? Why? Didn't we realise the danger? Did we have any weapons? Who was the foreigner? Why was he interested in a man-eating leopard from seventy years ago? After about ten minutes we were allowed through, having promised not to stay too long, or discuss the political situation with the local people, or report on it when we left. The armed soldiers left us in no doubt that they thought we were crazy.

Finally we drove into the village of Punanai. At the edge of the road there was a ramshackle stall selling ginger tea. We stopped to talk to some of the villagers and I couldn't help but notice the guns lying in the grass nearby. I drank in silence, nervous and glad to have something to do with my hands, but Raja chatted easily enough with the young men. We ordered a second cup and Raja asked if they had ever heard a story of a man-eating leopard or its slayer, Shelton Agar? We were met with quizzical expressions all around and the discussion quickly turned back to the Tigers. But from the corner of my eye I could see an old man dozing in the shade who looked up, rather startled, at Raja's words. At first he seemed an incongruous figure amongst the Tamil occupants of the roadside stall. 'Let's ask him,' I suggested.

The old man's story that followed provided vital information for the historical element of my book. His actual words never made it into print; my editors deemed them too outlandish, too shocking. But this old

1 Liberation Tigers of Tamil Elam

man shifted my understanding of those events eighty years ago from a man-versus-beast adventure story to something altogether more chilling. No matter how much my editors scoffed, I could not dismiss the old man so easily. They had not seen the certainty in his eyes or caught the sharpness of his memory. Perhaps too they had not seen as many inexplicable events as I had.

"I saw Kuveni," said the old man. There was a pause while he registered our blank looks. He narrowed his eyes and looked at me closely, as though weighing me up before shrugging and carrying on. "Ah. You do not know. What I mean is that I saw the leopard, the man-eater. I was there."

When Raja softly translated this to me, I could hardly contain my excitement. A hundred questions rushed into my mind, threatening to spill out, but Raja urged caution. We should let the old man tell his own story at his own pace; there was more to be learned by listening. So I simply nodded. Raja smiled at the old man and gently asked him to tell us more of what he knew.

"I was working on the railway, on the extension between Batticaloa and Trincomalee. All my friends had jobs on the tracks. It was good work at first, hard labour, but satisfying and friendly too. There was a good feeling about the railway, that we were building something useful. In the evenings people would tell old tales from the Mahavansa. It was like a competition to see who could spin the best story. My friend, Ananda, he was the champion. You could almost see the characters flickering on the edges of the fire's shadows when he spoke. He made them so real. He made me want to learn about our myths, our history. And I did, after . . . after the man-eater, as you call her. But no one ever brought a story to life like Ananda. Not until that day.

"Anyway, the mood on the tracks soon changed. One day a man went

"I saw Kuveni," said the old man. "Ah. You do not know. What I mean is that I saw the leopard, the man-eater. I was there."

missing. Then another. We searched and searched but found nothing. Then a third man. This time we found a body, all the soft insides were chewed out. Then the rumours started flying. It was a monster, a leopard, and a beast that could appear from nowhere – a flash of white gold in the grasses – and could vanish just as fast. The camp was a different place – everyone looking over his shoulder. No jokes, no chatter.

"The last evening story that Ananda told, he may have embellished perhaps, but we all heard it, we all heard its truth. We carried it with us every day, just as I still do. There were no more tales from the Mahavansa after that. Some of my friends started sleeping in the tree branches to be safer. I am not ashamed to say I was scared . . . only a fool pretends he isn't afraid. I went to the witch doctor – the vederala – and talked of what was going on, of that last story. He gave me this."

The old man held up a pendant hanging round his neck. It was a *divi-niya-pota* – two leopard claws mounted in silver with filigree decoration. "I wear it for protection. And I always carried this with me." He pulled a large knife from his waist. "I did what I could to protect myself, but all around men were panicking, wondering if they would be next. Some were so scared they almost went crazy. Some left altogether – they'd rather give up their wages than stay. And it wasn't just us. Villagers were taken too. By the time Manickam went, we'd lost nineteen to the leopard."

"Who is Manickam?" asked one of the young men. We weren't the only audience now. The measured intensity of the old man's voice and the gory mystery of his story had drawn in our companions.

"He was the Inspector's servant. The Inspector, Altendorff was his name, he came to look at the track – check its safety, our progress, check up on us. He sent Manickam to post his letters, but the fool took a short-cut. I didn't see the body that day, not until later. We were working to clear the tall grass from the side of the road that morning. Hot work, but vital – we didn't want the creature to have anywhere to hide. Altendorff came running up in a frenzy. Before he could get his breath back even he had picked four of us – the strongest ones with the biggest knives I think! He led us back, cutting a trail though the undergrowth further into the jungle. You could see the blood on the ground. Every step was leading us closer to the danger. It was crazy. After a while the four of us stopped. We refused to go on. To carry on any further would have been certain death and the Inspector must have known it too. We were all back at the road soon enough, shaking with relief. And then I think the Inspector must have sent a telegram because soon another man came, Captain Agar."

At the mention of this name, Raja asked the old man to pause, to allow him to give me the gist of the story so far. I mentioned that it was only by coincidence that Shelton Agar saw that telegram, and that he just happened to be passing through Batticaloa when the news came in. I said to Raja: "Can you ask him if he knows that Agar had tried to kill the leopard before?"

The old man suddenly seemed to lose interest and I was worried that I had offended him with my interruption and had broken the flow of reminiscence. I motioned for him to continue and swore to myself I would not interrupt again. Thankfully, as the old man reached the heart of the story, he seemed to drift even further into the past. His gaze was fixed somewhere, as though he could see the characters of his youth acting out their deadly adventure once more in the middle distance.

"Oh yes," said the old man. "We had all heard about the great captain's battle to slay the leopard. He tried to trap her using a goat as bait, but of course she was much too cunning for that. I wasn't surprised to see him back – he was pleased to have another chance. I knew there was a reward offered for killing the man-eater, but I don't think it was the money that drove him. A man like that didn't need any more money and he didn't have that lust for money in his eyes. No, he had a lust for danger. It was something personal for him to get the better of the creature. It seemed as though he thought about the leopard all the time. He was so determined.

"The Captain and the Inspector took us into the bush again. I nearly refused to go, but I was young then – I wanted my share of the glory, and I had my talisman. Again we walked close to Manickam's trail of blood. One of my friends cleared our way ahead. Then came the Captain, another worker, the Captain's driver, then me and the Inspector and a fourth worker behind us. Each of us holding our breath. I remember all I could hear was the swish of the path being cleared ahead and the irritating buzz of all those flies. Then we saw the body. I have seen the remains of many animals killed by predators, and I have seen the bodies of men killed by other men too, but this . . . this was the devil's work. The corpse was propped up against a pallu tree like a doll, like someone stopping to take a rest in the shade, but it was naked, tattered clothes strewn about and the neck was bitten horribly. One of his legs was mostly gone, and his belly, eaten out, trailing across the ground. I nearly ran then. The beast hadn't finished and she couldn't be far. But the Captain, he was so excited. He ordered us to build an ambush and wait. Ah, so much waiting!

"The waiting was almost the worst part. Standing in silence, pictures of the body before my eyes, imagining Manickam's last moments, the knowledge of Kuveni's power growing in my mind. The white men couldn't know anything of this, but even they were tense, though they made such a show of not showing it. By the time we heard a low growl close by we were all so jumpy that the Captain dropped his cigarette. He ordered us to shoot to kill, but the clever creature wouldn't show herself.

"It was starting to rain and sunset was coming. The Captain insisted we go back to the village for food and lanterns to prepare to wait through the night. It was my job to tie the body to the tree so that the beast couldn't drag it away. I can still feel the roughness of the rope in my hand – to use a human as bait – and the stickiness of the blood. I was trying to secure the wrists without having to look too closely when I sensed it. Danger. Something in the air, more than the knowledge of a predator nearby. I was familiar with that sensation. You too, perhaps. But this

THE MAN-EATER OF PUNANAI

was something more than that, darker even than that. An older kind of fear that I can't describe. She must have been watching us all afternoon, but this was the first time I felt her close. I ran and didn't see what exactly happened. The Inspector fired first, I think, and then the Captain. He might even have caught her, but still she . . . vanished.

"We went back to camp and returned when the sky was black. The Captain, who seemed to want to risk all our lives, went up to the tree to inspect the bait. But it was gone. The body I had tied so securely was gone. That was the only time I saw fear on his face. It must have been obvious by then even to him that this was a leopard unlike any other. We hurried back to safety for the night.

"I thought they might give up after that, but the next morning the Captain was more determined than ever before. I felt a sick feeling of foreboding. I wanted to be able to tell them what we all knew, but I knew I would never be believed. There was no point. So we went back once more and this time followed the trail of the body where it had been dragged from the tree. We found a skull with just a few strips of flesh still attached. And then a crunching noise coming from the bush. Everyone started moving at once, most of us away from the sound, the Captain striding towards it, his gun at the ready. My friend thought he saw her and shot, but it was only a sambur.

"The Captain was looking crazed by now. He wanted us to build another platform about ten feet above the ground, where he could hide. The seat and the platform were ready by mid-morning and we dragged the body – what was left of it – to a small clearing nearby. It was rotting by now, covered in flies. Then we walked away. Two took up posts in the surrounding trees and I stood watch at the bottom of a tree some distance from the bait, leaving the Captain on his platform near the ambush. It was the same as the day before: waiting, fear, silence, thirst. Only the sound of mosquitoes for conversation. I wondered what the Captain was thinking. Had his imagination, like mine, played through all the possible, terrible outcomes of this crazy scheme? Did he think he saw the leopard each time the light shifted over the leaves beneath him? Was he startled by the sudden noises of the jungle – a bird's shriek, the trees creaking? He must have been sweating now, anticipating an attack at any moment, standing so still, so close to the stinking remains of a man whose fate could so easily be his own. But this Captain always seemed more excited than afraid. Perhaps he did not recognise the man-eater as I did; perhaps he had his own God to guide him.

"I remember the Inspector left his post in the afternoon to fetch tea. That was a reckless journey in itself. Who knew where the beast could be hiding? But he was loyal to his fellow Englishman and the Captain must have had a terrible thirst. When he got back the rain started. I sensed something – power. I should have climbed then, but I was paralysed with fear. She was there, about thirty feet away. The leopard. Staring across at me, baring her fangs, swinging her tail. Her eyes were golden. I had time to think how magnificent she was before I panicked. Then I was reaching up, those eyes fixed in my mind, my hands scrabbling on the wet bark trying to haul myself up the tree and out of danger before she could reach me."

The old man paused for breath and his audience breathed with him, all of us transfixed by his words and by what might come next. But he said nothing for some moments, simply pulling back the cloth of his sarong to reveal his leg beneath. A series of ragged, pale scars stretched along the outside of his thigh, almost from his hip bone, twisting round to the back of the knee. The skin was white and corrugated, standing out against the soft, wrinkled flesh surrounding it. A gruesome scar.

"My talisman was not working for me that day," the old man continued. "Just as I was reaching for a higher branch and safety I felt her claws pierce my skin, pulling downwards to scrape the bone, tearing away my flesh. It was so quick and such a shock I do not think I realised quite what had happened before I turned and saw my blood, my own

The stuffed carcase of the man-eater of Punanai is still in the Colombo Museum.

blood, on the ground. I screamed then. Somehow I managed to pull myself up again, before she could lunge once more. I did not feel the pain until later. Then I heard a shot.

"My scream had alerted the others and somehow the Captain had got an angle on the beast. He shot her in the heart through her neck. They say it was a very fine shot although I did not see, of course. Perhaps my talisman was with me after all – the only man to have survived an encounter with the man-eater. They rushed me back to camp for medical treatment and I recovered relatively quickly from the wound. It took longer to stop dreaming about it, to stop seeing those eyes, feeling the points of her claws again and again. Everyone else thought that was that: the man-eater dead, the Captain a hero. But perhaps he sensed more than he knew. I heard it said later that he had described the leopard as 'some beautiful white devil.' Those were his words, 'beautiful white devil.' And so she was."

★ ★ ★

As he finished speaking there was silence. The youngsters lounging around the tea stall, their own guns only a few feet away, were looking at the old man with new respect. When Raja quietly translated the end of the tale for me, I could hardly believe that I was sitting in the presence not just of a man who had seen the man-eater, but who had been there at its death – a man who had been wounded by it and miraculously survived. Perhaps I should not have been so surprised by my editors' doubts over including this episode in my book. If I hadn't heard for myself the old man's tale and seen the scars I would not have believed it. Listening to the old man, I knew he was speaking the truth, although I was sure that there was still some mystery he was holding back.

"Ask him about Kuveni," I begged Raja. "And what was the story his friend told on that last night at the campsite?"

After some hurried conversation during which the old man seemed reluctant to tell more, he eventually spoke again.

"My friend, Ananda, told the story of Kuveni. I cannot tell it like he did and you cannot understand how significant it was at that time . . ." There was a long pause. "Kuveni was the queen of the Yakkas, and a witch too. The Yakkas were famous for being able to transform themselves into other forms, other animals. She seduced Vijaya, the founder of our race. Their children became the Veddas, the primitive tribe who still live nearby.

"After some years, Vijaya banished her and married a beautiful princess instead. Kuveni was furious. She wanted to kill him. Using her powers of witchcraft she became a leopard and prowled into his bedroom. But Vijaya was protected by his guards, so Kuveni stuck out her long tongue, a tongue made of crystal, to curse him with its touch. A soldier cut off the tongue and put it in a golden box. But it was too late. The tongue became a leopard again, and when the box was open it fled into the night. The king never recovered from the curse and died with no children. That is the *divi dos*, the curse of the she-devil.

"When we heard the story, we knew the truth of it. The man-eater was not a leopard such as you or I have seen before. And Captain Agar sensed that too. It was the she-devil, the *divi dos*. He may have killed the beast, but the curse lives on. Look around you. It is plain to see. The curse lives on."

CHAPTER 7

A Passion in the Desert
(Une Passion dans le désert)

HONORÉ DE BALZAC
Translated by
J. N. O. RUDD, BA

Balzac's original name was Honoré Balssa. He was born on 20 May 1799 in Tours, France, and died in Paris on 18 August 1850. A French literary artist, Balzac produced a vast number of novels and short stories collectively called La Comédie Humaine (The Human Comedy). He helped to establish the orthodox classical novel and is generally considered to be one of the greatest fiction writers of all time.

"The sight was fearful!" she cried, as we quit M. Martin's menagerie.

She had seen that fearless wild-beast tamer going through his marvellous performance in a cage of hyenas.

"How can it be possible," she went on, "to so tame those creatures as to be sure of them?"

"It is an enigma to you," I replied, "yet still it is naturally a fact."

"Ah!" she exclaimed, her lips quivering incredulously.

"You think, then, that beasts are without feeling?" I asked. "Be assured by me that they are taught by us all of our vices and virtues – those of civilization."

Amazement was expressed in her look.

"At the time I first saw Monsieur Martin, I, like you, exclaimed my amazement," I went on. "It happened that I was seated alongside an old soldier, his right leg amputated, who had attracted my notice by his appearance as I went into the show. His face showed the dauntless look of the Napoleonic wars, disfigured as it was with battle scars. This old hero, beside, had a frank, jolly style which, wherever I come across it, is always attractive to me. Undoubtedly he was one of those old campaigners who are surprised at nothing, who can make a jest on the last grimaces of a dying comrade, or will bury his friend or rifle his body with gaiety; give a challenge to every bullet with composure; make a short shriving for himself or others; and usually, as the rule goes, fraternizing with the devil. He closely watched the proprietor of the exhibition as he entered the cage, curling his lip, that peculiar sign of contemptuous satire which better informed men assume to signify how superior they are to the dupes. The veteran smiled when I exclaimed at the cool daring of Monsieur Martin, he gave a toss of the head, and, with a knowing grimace, said: 'An old game!'

" 'Old game,' said I, 'what do you mean? You will greatly oblige me if you can explain the secret of the mysterious power of this man.'"

"We came to be acquainted after a while and went to dine at the first café we saw after quitting the menagerie. After a bottle of champagne with our dessert, which burnished up his memory and rendered it very vivid, he narrated a circumstance in his early history which showed very conclusively that he had ample reason to style Monsieur Martin's performance 'an old game.'"

When we arrived at her house she so teased me, and was withal so charming, making me a number of so pretty promises, that I consented to write the yarn narrated by the veteran hero for her behoof. On the morrow I sent her this adventure, which might well be headed: 'The French in Egypt'.

*   *   *

During the expedition to Upper Egypt under General Desaix, a Provencal soldier, who had fallen into the clutches of the Maugrabins, was marched by these marauders, these tireless Arabs, into the deserts lying beyond the cataracts of the Nile.

So as to put a sufficient distance between themselves and the French army, to insure their greater safety, the Maugrabins made forced marches and rested only during the night. They then encamped around a well shaded by palm trees, under which they had previously concealed a store of provisions. Never dreaming that their prisoner would think of escaping, they satisfied themselves by merely tying his hands, then lay down to sleep, after having regaled themselves on a few dates and given provender to their horses.

When the courageous Provencal noted that they slept soundly and could no longer watch his movements, he made use of his teeth to steal a scimitar, steadied the blade between his knees, cut through the thongs which bound his hands. In an instant he was free. He at once seized a carbine and a long dirk, then took the precaution of providing himself with a stock of dried dates, a small bag of oats, some powder and bullets, and hung a scimitar around his waist, mounted one of the horses and spurred on in the direction in which he supposed the French army to be. So impatient was he to see a bivouac again that he pressed on the already tired courser at such a speed that its flanks were lacerated with the spurs, and soon the poor animal, utterly exhausted, fell dead, leaving the Frenchman alone in the midst of the desert.

After walking for a long time in the sand, with all the courage and firmness of an escaped convict, the soldier was obliged to stop, as the day had already come to an end. Despite the beauty of an Oriental night, with its exquisite sky, he felt that he could not, though he fain would, continue on his weary way. Fortunately he had come to a small eminence, on the summit of which grew a few palm trees whose verdure shot into the air and could be seen from afar; this had brought hope and consolation to his heart.

His fatigue was so great that he threw himself down on a block of granite, capriciously fashioned by nature into the semblance of a camp-bed, and, without taking any precaution for defence, was soon fast in sleep. He had made the sacrifice of his life. His last waking thought was one of regret. He repented having left the Maugrabins, whose nomad life seemed to smile on him now that he was far from them and from all hope of succour.

He was awakened by the sun, whose pitiless rays fell with their intensest heat on the granite, and produced a most intolerable sense of torridness – for he had most stupidly placed himself inversely to the shadow cast by the verdant and majestic fronds of the palm trees. He looked at these solitary monarchs and shuddered – they reminded him of the graceful shafts crowned with waving foliage which characterize the Sarracenic columns in the Cathedral of Aries.

But when, after counting the palm trees, he cast his eyes around him, the most horrible despair took possession of his soul. The dark, forbidding sands of the desert spread farther than sight could reach in every direction, and glittered with a dull lustre like steel struck by light. It was a limitless ocean that he saw. It might have been a sea of ice or a chain of lakes that lay mirrored around him. A fiery vapour carried in streaks formed perpetual heat waves over this heaving continent. The sky was glowing with an Oriental splendor of insupportable translucence, disappointing, inasmuch as it leaves naught for the imagination to exceed. Heaven, earth, both were on fire.

The silence was awful in its wild, tremendous majesty. Infinitude, immensity, closed in upon the soul from every side. Not a cloud in the sky, not a breath in the air, not a rift on the bosom of the sand, which was ever moving in ever-diminishing wavelets, scarcely disturbing the surface; the horizon fell into space, traced by a slim line of light, definite as the edge of a sabre – like as in summer seas a beam of light just divides the earth from the heaven which meets it.

The Provencal threw his arms around the trunk of one of the palm trees, as though it were the body of a friend; and there, in the shelter of its slender, straight shadow cast by it upon the granite, he wept. Then sitting down he remained motionless, contemplating with awful dread the implacable scene which Nature stretched out before him. He cried aloud to measure the solitude. His voice, lost in the hollows of the hillocks, sounded in the distance with a faint resonance, but aroused no echo – the echo was in the soldier's heart. The Provencal was two-and-twenty; he loaded his carbine.

"Time enough yet," he muttered to himself, laying on the ground the weapon which alone could give him deliverance.

Looking by turns at the burnished black expanse and the blue immensity of the sky, the soldier dreamed of France – he smelt with delight, in his longing fancy, the gutters of Paris – he remembered the towns through which he had passed, the faces of his fellow soldiers, the most trivial incidents of his life.

His southern imagination saw the stones of his dearly loved Provence in the undulating play of the heat which spread in waves over the out-spread sheet of the desert. Fearing the dangers of this so cruel mirage, he went down the opposite side of the knoll to that up which he had come on the previous day. How great was his joy when he discerned a natural grotto, formed of immense blocks of granite, the foundation of the rising ground. The remains of a rug showed that this place had at one time been inhabited; a short distance therefrom were some date-palms laden with fruit. There arose in his heart that instinct which binds us to life. He now hoped to live long enough to see the passing of some wandering Arabs, who should pass that way; perhaps, who should say, he might hear the sound of cannon; for at that time Bonaparte was traversing Egypt.

These thoughts inspired him with new life. The palm tree near him seemed to bend under its weight of ripe fruit. The Frenchman shook down some of the clusters, and, when he tasted the unhoped-for manna, he felt convinced that the palms had been cultivated by some former inhabitant – the rich and luscious flavour of the fresh meat of the dates were attestations of the care of his unknown predecessor. As like all Provencals, he passed from the gloom of dark despair to an almost insane joy.

He went up again, running, to the top of the hillock, where he devoted the remainder of the day to cutting down one of the sterile palm trees which, the previous night, had served him as a shelter. A vague memory made him think of the wild beasts of the desert. He foresaw that they would most likely come to drink at the spring which was visible, bubbling through the sand, at the base of the rock, but lost itself in the desert farther down. He resolved to guard himself against their unwelcome visits to his hermitage by felling a tree which should fall across the entrance.

Despite his diligence and the strength which the dread of being devoured in his sleep lent him, he was unable to cut the palm tree in pieces during the day, but he was successful in felling it. At eventide the monarch of the desert tumbled down; the noise of its falling resounded far and wide like a moan from Solitude's bosom; the soldier shuddered as though he heard a voice predicting evil.

But like an heir who mourns not his parent's decease, he stripped off from this beautiful tree the arching green fronds, its poetic adornment, and used them in forming his couch on which to rest.

Fatigued by his labours, he soon fell asleep under the red vault of his damp, cool cave.

In the middle of the night his sleep was disturbed by an extraordinary sound. He sat up; the profound silence that reigned around enabled him to distinguish the alternating rhythm of a respiration whose savage energy it was impossible could be that of a human being.

A terrible terror, increased yet more by the silence, the darkness, his racing fancy, froze his heart within him. He felt his hair rise on end, as his eyes, dilated to their utmost, perceived through the gloom two faint amber lights. At first he attributed these lights to the delusion of his vision, but presently the vivid brilliance of the night aided him to gradually distinguish the objects around him in the cave, when he saw, within the space of two feet of him, a huge animal lying at rest. Was it a lion? Was it a tiger? Was it a crocodile?

The Provencal was not sufficiently well educated to know under what sub-species his enemy should be classed; his fear was but the greater because his ignorance led him to imagine every terror at once. He endured most cruel tortures as he noted every variation of the breathing which was so near him; he dared not make the slightest movement.

An odour, pungent like that of a fox, but more penetrating as it were, more profound, filled the cavern. When the Provencal became sensible of this, his terror reached the climax, for now he could no longer doubt the proximity of a terrible companion, whose royal lair he had utilized as a bivouac.

Presently the reflection of the moon, as it slowly descended to the horizon, lighted up the den, rendering gradually visible the gleaming, resplendent, and spotted skin of a panther.

This lion of Egypt lay asleep curled up like a great dog, the peaceful possessor of a kennel at the door of some sumptuous hotel; its eyes opened for a moment, then closed again; its face was turned toward the Frenchman. A thousand confused thoughts passed through the mind of the tiger's prisoner. Should he, as he at first thought of doing, kill it with a shot from his carbine? But he saw plainly that there was not room enough in which to take proper aim; the muzzle would have extended beyond the animal – the bullet would miss the mark. And what if it were to wake! – This fear kept him motionless and rigid.

He heard the pulsing of his heart beating in the so dread silence and he cursed the too violent pulsations which his surging blood brought on, lest they should awaken from sleep the dreadful creature; that slumber which gave him time to think and plan over his escape.

Twice did he place his hand upon his scimitar, intending to cut off his enemy's head; but the difficulty of severing the close-haired skin caused him to renounce this daring attempt. To miss was *certain* death. He preferred the chances of a fair fight, and made up his mind to await the daylight. The dawn did not give him long to wait. It came.

He could now examine the panther at his ease; its muzzle was smeared with blood.

"It's had a good dinner," he said, without troubling himself to speculate whether the feast might have been of human flesh or not. "It won't be hungry when it wakes."

It was a female. The fur on her belly and thighs was glistening white. Many small spots like velvet formed beautiful bracelets round her paws; her sinuous tail was also white, ending in black rings. The back of her dress was yellow, like unburnished gold, very lissome and soft, and had the characteristic blotches in the shape of pretty rosettes, which distinguished the panther from every other species *felis*.

This formidable hostess lay tranquilly snoring in an attitude as graceful and easy as that of a cat on the cushions of an ottoman. Her bloody paws, nervous and well armed, were stretched out before her head, which rested on the back of them, while from her muzzle radiated her straight, slender whiskers, like threads of silver.

If he had seen her lying thus, imprisoned in a cage, the Provencal would doubtless have admired the grace of the creature and the vivid contrasts of colour which gave her robe an imperial splendour; but just then his sight was jaundiced by sinister forebodings.

The presence of the panther, even asleep, had the same effect upon him as the magnetic eyes of a snake are said to have on the nightingale.

The soldier's courage oozed away in the presence of this silent danger, though he was a man who gathered courage at the mouths of cannon belching forth shot and shell. And yet a bold thought brought daylight to his soul and sealed up the source from whence issued the cold sweat which gathered on his brow. Like men driven to bay, who defy death and offer their bodies to the smiter, so he, seeing in this merely a tragic episode, resolved to play his part with honour to the last.

"The day before yesterday," said he, "the Arabs might have killed me."

So considering himself as already dead, he waited bravely, but with anxious curiosity, the awakening of his enemy.

When the sun appeared the panther suddenly opened her eyes; then she stretched out her paws with energy, as if to get rid of cramp. Presently she yawned and showed the frightful armament of her teeth, and the pointed tongue rough as a rasp.

"She is like a dainty woman," thought the Frenchman, seeing her rolling and turning herself about so softly and coquettishly. She licked off the blood from her paws and muzzle, and scratched her head with reiterated grace of movement.

"Good, make your little toilet," said the Frenchman to himself; he recovered his gaiety with his courage. "We are presently about to give each other good morning," and he felt for the short poniard that he had abstracted from the Maugrabins. At this instant the panther turned her head toward him and gazed fixedly at him, without otherwise moving.

The rigidity of her metallic eyes and their insupportable lustre made him shudder. The beast approached him; he looked at her caressingly, staring into those bright eyes in an effort to magnetize her – to soothe her. He let her come quite close to him before stirring; then with a movement both gentle and amorous, as though he were caressing the most beautiful of women, he passed his hand over her whole body, from the head to the tail, scratching the flexible vertebrae, which divided the yellow back of the panther. The animal slightly moved her tail voluptuously, and her eyes grew soft and gentle; and when for the third time the Frenchman had accomplished this interested flattery, she gave vent to those purrings like as cats express their pleasure; but it issued from a throat so deep, so powerful, that it resounded through the cave like the last chords of an organ rolling along the vaulted roof of a church. The Provencal, seeing the value of his caresses, redoubled them until they completely soothed and lulled this imperious courtesan.

When he felt assured that he had extinguished the ferocity of his capricious companion, whose hunger had so luckily been appeased the day before, he got up to leave the grotto. The panther let him go out, but when he reached the summit of the little knoll she sprang up and bounded after him with the lightness of a sparrow hopping from twig to twig on a tree, and rubbed against his legs, arching her back after the manner of a domestic cat. Then regarding her guest with eyes whose glare had somewhat softened, she gave vent to that wild cry which naturalists compare to the grating of a saw.

"Madame is exacting," said the Frenchman, smiling.

He was bold enough to play with her ears; he stroked her belly and scratched her head good and hard with his nails. He was encouraged with his success, and tickled her skull with the point of his dagger, watching for an opportune moment to kill her, but the hardness of the bone made him tremble, dreading failure.

The sultana of the desert showed herself gracious to her slave; she lifted her head, stretched out her neck, and betrayed her delight by the tranquillity of her relaxed attitude. It suddenly occurred to the soldier that, to slay this savage princess with one blow, he must stab deep in the throat.

He raised the blade, when the panther, satisfied, no doubt, threw herself gracefully at his feet and glanced up at him with a look in which, despite her natural ferocity, a glimmer of good will was apparent. The poor Provencal, thus frustrated for the nonce, ate his dates as he leaned against one of the palm trees, casting an interrogating glance from time to time across the desert, in quest of some deliverer, and on his terrible companion, watching the chances of her uncertain clemency.

The panther looked at the place where the date stones fell; and, each time he threw one, she examined the Frenchman with an eye of commercial distrust. However, the examination seemed to be favourable to him, for, when he had eaten his frugal meal, she licked his boots with her powerful, rough tongue, cleaning off the dust which was caked in the wrinkles in a marvellous manner.

"Ah! but how when she is really hungry?" thought the Provencal. In spite of the shudder caused by this thought, his attention was curiously drawn to the symmetrical proportions of the animal, which was certainly one of the most splendid specimens of its race. He began to measure them with his eye. She was three feet in height at the shoulders and four feet in length, not counting her tail; this powerful weapon was nearly three feet long, and rounded like a cudgel. The head, large as that of a lioness, was distinguished by an intelligent, crafty expression. The cold cruelty of the tiger dominated, and yet it bore a vague resemblance to the face of a wanton woman. Indeed, the countenance of this solitary queen had something of the gaiety of a Nero in his cups; her thirst for blood was slaked, now she wished for amusement.

The soldier tried if he might walk up and down, the panther left him freedom, contenting herself with following him with her eyes, less

The fur on her belly and thighs was glistening white. Many small spots like velvet formed beautiful bracelets round her paws; her sinuous tail was also white, ending in black rings. The back of her dress was yellow, like unburnished gold, very lissome and soft, and had the characteristic blotches and the shape of pretty rosettes.

like a faithful dog watching his master's movements with affectionate solicitude, than a huge Angora cat uneasy and suspicious of every movement.

When he looked around he saw, by the spring, the carcase of his horse; the panther had dragged the remains all that distance, and had eaten about two-thirds of it already. The sight reassured the Frenchman, it made it easy to explain the panther's absence and the forbearance she had shown him while he slept.

This first good luck emboldened the soldier to think of the future. He conceived the wild idea of continuing on good terms with his companion and to share her home, to try every means to tame her, and endeavoring to turn her good graces to his account.

With these thoughts he returned to her side, and had the unspeakable joy of seeing her wag her tail with an almost imperceptible motion as he approached. He sat down beside her, fearlessly, and they began to play together. He took her paws and muzzle, twisted her ears, rolled her over on her back, and stroked her warm, delicate flanks. She allowed him to do whatever he liked, and, when he began to stroke the fur on her feet, she carefully drew in her murderously savage claws, which were sharp and curved like a Damascus sword.

The Frenchman kept one hand on his poniard, and thought to watch his chance to plunge it into the belly of the too confiding animal; but he was fearful lest he might be strangled in her last convulsive struggles; beside this, he felt in his heart a sort of remorse which bade him respect this hitherto inoffensive creature that had done him no hurt. He seemed to have found a friend in the boundless desert, and, half-unconsciously, his mind reverted to his old sweetheart whom he had, in derision, nicknamed "Mignonne" by way of contrast because she was so furiously jealous; during the whole period of their intercourse he lived in dread of the knife with which she ever threatened him.

This recollection of his youthful days suggested the idea of making the panther answer to this name, now that he began to admire with less fear her graceful swiftness, agility, and softness. Toward the close of the day he had so familiarized himself with his perilous position that he was half in love with his dangerous situation and its painfulness. At last his companion had grown so far tamed that she had caught the habit of looking up at him whenever he called in a falsetto voice "Mignonne."

At the setting of the sun Mignonne, several times in succession, gave a long, deep, melancholy cry.

"She has been well brought up," thought the light-hearted soldier; "she says her prayers." But this jesting thought only occurred to him when he noticed that his companion still retained her pacific attitude.

"Come, my little blonde, I'll let you go to bed first," he said to her, counting on the activity of his own legs to run away as soon as she was asleep; to reach as great distance as possible, and seek some other shelter for the night.

With the utmost impatience the soldier waited the hour of his flight. When it arrived he started off vigorously in the direction of the Nile; but hardly had he made a quarter of a league in the sand when he heard the panther bounding after him; at intervals giving out that saw-like cry which was more terrible than her leaping gait.

"Ah!" said he, "she's fallen in love with me; she has never met any one before; it is really flattering to be her first love."

So thinking he fell into one of those treacherous quicksands, so menacing to travellers, and from which it is an impossibility to save one's self. Finding himself caught he gave a shriek of alarm. The panther seizing his collar with her teeth, and, springing vigorously backward, drew him as by magic out of the sucking sand.

"Ah, Mignonne!" cried the soldier, enthusiastically kissing her; "we are bound to each other now – for life and death! But no tricks, mind!" and he retraced his steps.

From that time the desert was inhabited for him. It contained a being to whom he could talk and whose ferocity was now lulled into gentleness, although he could not explain to himself this strange friendship.

Anxious as he was to keep awake and on guard, as it were, he gradually succumbed to his excessive fatigue of body and mind; he threw himself on the floor of the cave and slept soundly.

On awakening Mignonne was absent; he climbed the hillock and afar off saw her returning in the long bounds characteristic of those animals, who cannot run owing to the extreme flexibility of the vertebral column.

Mignonne arrived with bloody jaws; she received the wonted caresses, the tribute her slave hastened to pay, and showed by her purring how transported she was. Her eyes, full of languor, rested more kindly on the Provencal than on the previous day, and he addressed her as he would have done a domestic animal.

"Ah! Mademoiselle, you're a nice girl, ain't you? Just see now! We like to be petted, don't we? Are you not ashamed of yourself? So you've been eating some Arab or other, eh? Well, that doesn't matter. They're animals, the same as you are; but don't take to crunching up a Frenchman, bear that in mind, or I shall not love you any longer."

She played like a dog with its master, allowing herself to be rolled over, knocked about, stroked, and the rest, alternately; at times she would coax him to play by putting her paw upon his knee and making a pretty gesture of solicitation.

Some days passed in this manner. This companionship allowed the Provencal to properly appreciate the sublime beauties of the desert. He had now discovered in the rising and setting of the sun sights utterly unknown to the world. He knew what it was to tremble when over his head he heard the hiss of a bird's wing, which occurred so rarely, or when he saw the clouds changing like many coloured travellers melting into each other. In the night-time he studied the effects of the moon upon the ocean of sand, where the simoon made waves swift of movement and rapid in their changes. He lived the life of the East; he marvelled at its wonderful pomp; then, after having reveled in the sight of a hurricane over the plain where the madly whirling sands made red, dry mists, and death-bearing clouds, he would welcome the night with joy, for then fell the blissful freshness of the light of the stars, and he listened to imaginary music in the skies.

Thus solitude taught him to unroll the treasures of dreams. He passed long hours in remembering mere nothings – trifles, and comparing his past life with the present.

In the end he grew passionately fond of his panther; for some sort of affection was a necessity.

Whether it was that his own will powerfully projected had modified that of his companion, or whether, because she had found abundant food in her predatory excursions in the desert, she respected the man's life, he feared no longer for it, for she became so exceedingly tame.

Most of his time he devoted to sleep, but he was compelled to watch like a spider in its web, that the moment of his deliverance might not escape him, in case any should come his way over that line marked by the horizon. His shirt he had sacrificed in the making of a flag, which he attached to the top of a palm tree from which he had torn the foliage. Taught by necessity, he found the means of keeping it spread out, by fastening twigs and wedges to the corners; for the fitful breeze might not be blowing at the moment when the passing traveler was looking over the desert.

Nevertheless there were long hours of gloom, when he had abandoned hope; then he played with his panther. He had come to understand the different inflexions of her voice, the expression of her eyes; he had studied the capricious patterns of the rosettes that marked her golden robe. Mignonne was not even angry when he took hold of the tuft at the end of her tail to count the black and white rings, those graceful ornaments which glistened in the sun like precious gems. It afforded him pleasure to contemplate the supple, lithe, soft lines of her lissome form, the whiteness of her belly, the graceful poise of her head. But it was especially when she was playing that he took the greatest pleasure in looking at her. The agility and youthful lightness of her movements were a continual wonder to him. He was amazed at the supple way in which she bounded, crept, and glided, or clung to the trunk of palm trees, or rolled over, crouching sometimes to the ground and gathering herself together for her mighty spring; how she washed herself and combed down her fur. He noted that however vigorous her spring might be, however slippery the block of granite upon which she landed, she would stop, motionless, at the one word 'Mignonne'.

One day, under a bright midday sun, a great bird hovered in the sky. The Provencal left his panther to gaze at this new guest; but after pausing for a moment the deserted sultana uttered a deep growl.

"God take me! I do believe that she is jealous," he cried, seeing the rigid look appearing again in the metallic eyes. "The soul of Virginie has passed into her body, that's sure!"

The eagle disappeared in the ether, and the soldier admired her again, recalled by the panther's evident displeasure, her rounded flanks, and the perfect grace of her attitude. She was as pretty as a woman. There was youth and grace in her form. The blonde fur of her robe shaded, with delicate gradations, to the dead white tones of her furry thighs; the vivid sunshine brought out in its fullness the brilliancy of this living gold and its variegated brown spots with indescribable lustre.

The Provencal and the panther looked at each other with a look pregnant with meaning. She trembled with delight (the coquettish creature) when she felt her friend scratch the strong bones of her skull with his nails. Her eyes glittered like lightning flashes – then she closed them tightly.

"She has a soul!" cried he, looking at the stillness of this queen of the sands, golden like them, white as their waving light, solitary and burning as themselves.

⋆　⋆　⋆

"Well," said she, "I have read your defence of the beasts, but now tell me the end of this friendship between two beings who seemed to understand each other so thoroughly."

"Ah! There you are!" I replied. "It finished as all great passions end – by a misunderstanding. I believe that both sides imagine treachery; pride prevents an explanation, the rupture comes to pass through obstinacy."

"And sometimes on pleasant occasions," said she, "a glance, a word, an exclamation is all-sufficient. Well, tell me the end of the story."

"That is horribly difficult. But you will understand it the better if I give it you in the words of the old veteran, as he finished the bottle of champagne and exclaimed:

"'I don't know how I could have hurt her, but she suddenly turned on me in a fury, seizing my thigh with her sharp teeth, and yet (I thought of this afterward) not cruelly. I imagined that she intended devouring me, and I plunged my poniard in her throat. She rolled over with a cry that rent my soul; she looked at me in her death struggle, but without anger. I would have given the whole world – my cross, which I had not yet gained, all, everything – to restore her life to her. It was as if I had assassinated a real human being, a friend. When the soldiers who had seen my flag came to my rescue they found me in tears. Ah! Well, monsieur,' he resumed, after a momentary pause, eloquent by its silence, 'I went through the wars in Germany, Spain, Russia, and France; I have marched my carcase well nigh the world over, but I have seen nothing comparable to the desert. Ah! It is most beautiful! Glorious!'

"'What were your feelings there?' I asked.

"'They cannot be told, young man. Besides, I do not always regret my panther, my bouquet of palms. I must, indeed, be sad for that. In the desert, you see, there is all and there is nothing.'

"'But wait! – Explain that!'

"'Well, then,' he replied, with an impatient gesture, 'God is there, man is not.'"

CHAPTER 8

The Riddle of Lewa Downs

CHRISTOPHER ONDAATJE

"Can the Ethiopian change his skin, or the leopard his spots?"
Jeremiah 13:23

A black leopard – a melanistic black panther – is one of the rarest animals in the world and one of the most difficult to see in the wild. The term melanistic comes from the word melanin, a dark coloured skin and hair pigment. Melanism in cats happens when there is an abnormal development of the pigment, resulting in the coat being very dark or black. Despite the unusual darkness, the leopard's spots can still be seen faintly, especially in bright sunlight. Melanism is hereditary, but not necessarily passed from one generation to the next, with individuals occurring in mixed litters.

Of course I have heard of black leopards being seen, and shot, in the jungles of southern India, particularly in the Kerala region and also in the Sinharaja rainforest of Sri Lanka. I have always wanted to see one and had once received a telephone call from Kerala to inform me that local herdsmen had trapped a black beast, known locally as 'the goat killer', in a deep pit. However, the animal died before I could get there.

Then in 1999 Nigel Winser of the Royal Geographical Society told me that a sighting of a black leopard had been reported on Lewa Downs on the northern foothills of Mount Kenya. The Lewa Ranch where the sighting had taken place – 40,000 acres of private land owned by the Craig family – is an enormous conservation area designed to protect elephants and other African game from poaching and human encroachment. The nearest town is Isiolo; beyond which is the vast and rugged expanse of Northern Kenya that reaches right up to the Ethiopian border. Much of Lewa Downs is more than 2,000 metres in elevation, interspersed with deep river valleys and enormous rocky outcroppings.

It was the end of November and although I wanted to drop everything to go to Lewa to search for the black leopard, I was involved in a film project in Sri Lanka with Canadian film director John McGreevy. This meant that I was committed to spending two gruelling weeks filming around Sri Lanka's ruined cities and the southeast Yala game sanctuary. I returned to England early in December and immediately made plans to fly to Kenya to stay with the Craig family, hoping against hope that I wasn't too late.

I didn't have much time, so, telephoning William Craig at the Lewa Ranch, I arranged for a trio of game trackers to do some preparatory work, looking for any signs of the black leopard in the twenty-five square kilometre area around where it had been sighted. Leopards are territorial animals and I was banking on my instinct that the cat would not have moved far in such a short space of time. I also thought that if the trackers could find recent pugmarks, or even a kill, my job would be a lot easier.

It was a long way to go on the basis of one unconfirmed sighting, but nonetheless I blocked out eight days to spend with the trackers looking for the leopard. I flew out of Heathrow Airport in England on the night of 8th December, arriving in Nairobi early the following day, before transferring to a small Cessna six-seater plane that got me to Lewa in time for lunch. I was greeted by my three trackers Mungai, Rikita and Alfred, who were happy to see me, but had no news of the leopard.

Mungai, a member of the Kikuyu tribe, was dressed in ordinary safari fatigues, but Rikita and Alfred, both Maasai, wore their faded red cotton cloaks slung over their shoulders. They were muscular, lean and beautiful, with their long ochre-stained hair carefully braided and gathered together, tied in a bunch and draped down their backs.

They were enthusiastic about the search, but not at all confident that we would find the black leopard. It was like finding a needle in a haystack, they said. Leopards are secretive, elusive and difficult to see at the best of times, but in December, after the 'short rains,' with the area much greener than usual, the task would be almost impossible.

Exhausted and jet-lagged, I decided to have a quick sleep before going out on a reconnaissance game drive in the early evening. The next thing

The Masai trackers wore faded red cloaks slung over their shoulders – they were muscular, lean and beautiful.

I knew Mungai, who was anxious to get going, was awakening me at five in the afternoon. I showered, had a cup of strong Kenyan coffee, got my camera equipment together and set off in the long wheel-base Land Rover that was to be mine for the next eight days.

Even though we were almost on the equator the fact that we were at 2,000 metres meant that it was quite cool. And so, wrapped up in my old leather jacket with a makeshift scarf around my neck and an old Montana hat, we coursed out away from the lodge, towards the Lewa River, making our way through the marshes and yellow fever trees, and back around the far side of Cave Hill towards the Ngare Ndare forest. It was about a thirty-kilometre circuit along the rough Lewa Downs roads. We drove almost the entire perimeter of the interior ranch speculating where we were to spend the next few days. We saw herds of elephant, the rare Grevy's zebra and the occasional group of reticulated giraffe that inhabit this part of northern Kenya. There were a few white rhinoceros and one small herd of eland, but there were no cats – no lions, no cheetahs and definitely no sign of a leopard.

Night falls quickly in Africa and soon after six o'clock it was too dark to see. So we returned to the ranch planning to start again before dawn the next day, when I planned to comb an area I had mapped out around the base of Cave Hill. It was wonderful to be back in the scrub forests of Africa.

∗   ∗   ∗

A black leopard – a melanistic black panther – is one of the rarest animals in the world and one of the most difficult to see in the wild. Usually encountered in the dense tropical rainforests of southeast Asia, the melanistic leopard's dark colouration gives it better camouflage where there is little sunlight. In drier, more desert-like areas, the regular leopard's golden spotted coat provides better concealment. It is widely believed that the black leopard is more vicious than its tawny counterpart, and this might be due to the level of acceptance into the litter – the black leopard has to fight harder for its place in the food chain.

In medieval times the black leopard was said to be friendly towards all animals except the dragon, which it lured to its fate by exuding a particularly sweet odour. Later it became a symbol of Christ until its savage nature became more widely known. It then became a symbol of evil and hypocritical flattery.

How the leopard got its spots is of course one of the all-time classics from Rudyard Kipling's *Just So Stories*. The story, one of my favourites, tells about life on the high veldt when all animals were much the same colour – either yellowish-greyish-brownish, or greyish-brownish-yellow-ish – with the result that, for the Ethiopian and the leopard, hunting the giraffe, zebra, eland, or kudu became a relatively easy matter. Although very one-sided, life went on until the giraffe, zebra, eland, and kudu moved away from the high veldt to the great forest area and gradually, over time, changed their uniform colour to a variety of blotches, stripes, and darker lines that made them blend into their new environment. This made hunting a very different matter for the Ethiopian and the leopard, as it became extremely difficult to recognise their prey. The two hunters went to the wise old baboon, which cryptically advised them to 'go into other spots as soon as you can.' Not understanding the message, and getting increasingly hungry, the two hunters eventually came to the forest area where the herbivores had settled.

The Ethiopian then decided that he, at any rate, was going to change the colour of his skin so that he could hide better in hollows and behind trees. The leopard, excited because he saw the Ethiopian change the colour of his skin, asked the Ethiopian to change his skin too, so that it would 'go into other spots'.

> 'Then the Ethiopian put his five fingers close together . . .
> and pressed them all over the Leopard, and wherever the
> five fingers touched they left five little black marks, all close
> together. You can see them on any Leopard's skin you like,
> Best Beloved. Sometimes the fingers slipped and the marks

got a little blurred; but if you look closely at any Leopard now you will see that there are always five spots . . .'

*　　*　　*

Mungai woke me again the following morning at five o'clock, out of a deep, deep sleep. It was very dark, and very cold. I was literally shivering when I hauled myself out of bed and quickly put on my safari clothes: long khaki trousers, a khaki shirt, two sweaters and my well worn walking boots. I shaved quickly, washed and drank some very strong black Kenyan coffee. There was no time to waste and I was out with my flashlight into the crisp morning air trying to find my way through the scrub to the courtyard where my two Maasai friends, Rikita and Alfred, were waiting in the Land Rover. I heaved all my camera equipment onto the back seat, and piled in beside Mungai who did the driving. We didn't say much apart from a short good morning greeting. It was far too cold.

In the morning darkness we drove silently out of the courtyard of Lewa Ranch, and out into the wilds of northern Kenya. The morning wind howled around us in the open vehicle. I was lucky to be sitting in front protected to some degree by the windscreen, and I could see Mungai crouched over the steering wheel peering into the darkness ahead of us. A guilt-ridden hyena furtively crossed the path in front of us, his eyes shining back at us reflecting our headlights. Occasionally we saw zebra moving towards the Lewa River for their morning drink. It was less than an hour before sunrise, but even then we could see that it was a cloudless sky.

Within half an hour we were crossing the plains at the foot of Cave Hill; and minutes later the morning light stretched across the eastern sky heralding the dawn. It was quite silent, apart from the Land Rover's engine disturbing the African morning. And then, just as the sun's golden ball crept over the horizon – towards Mount Kenya whose outline we could just make out – came the morning chorus. Three crowned cranes perched high on a spreading umbrella acacia; the high-pitched screech of an African tawny eagle and the plaintive call of an African bou-bou. The world was coming to life: Bateleur eagles soared overhead, and we disturbed a sleeping Verreaux eagle owl.

There are few places in the world as beautiful as Africa in the morning. In the early light we could just make out the silhouette of a small herd of eland on the eastern slopes opposite Cave Hill. There were more zebras, both Grevy's and Burchells, now visible on the plains. The sun came up quickly and the sky gave up its russet morning glow and turned to bright blue. I suppose my Maasai companions were used to days like this, but to me it was spellbinding. We continued on our morning survey: down into the valleys and marsh, under the spreading umbrella acacias and candelabra euphorbia, out again onto open plains and then back to the river where more animals had gathered to drink. Two ostriches strutted along the river road in front of us, oblivious to our mission.

An hour later we stopped for coffee, when quite suddenly we heard the alarm call from an impala (we hadn't seen any that morning), and then the deep guttural sawing noise of a predator. "Leopard," said Mungai, listening with one ear to the caves above the plain. And then again we heard the unmistakable insistent grating noise of an adult leopard. We waited for a few minutes and drove on. "That was definitely a leopard," I said, and then thinking again, ordered Mungai to stop. He turned off the engine. We listened expectantly, but heard nothing.

I was certain that we had heard a leopard and my two Maasai trackers agreed, particularly Rikita, but it was impossible without seeing it to say that it was the black leopard. I was certain that the sound had come from high up on Cave Hill. We returned to the spot from where we first heard it, and listened again. Still nothing. After a few silent minutes Mungai was in favour of continuing our drive through the canyons.

"Listen," I said. "If there is a chance that this is the black leopard, we must surround the hill and hope that he shows himself. We have to gamble."

I suggested that Rikita wait secluded and hidden in the long brown grass at the foot of Cave Hill, and that Alfred sit higher up on the western rim of the hill. The Maasai, as I later learned, have incredible patience. The sun was high in the sky now, and I had asked them to expose themselves in the hot African sun for the greater part of the day. I gave my binoculars to Rikita, and the two Maasai youths silently slipped out of the Land Rover, and across the plain to their lookout position. This was about a kilometre from where Mungai and I stationed ourselves on a hillock overlooking the entire south face of Cave Hill.

It was only eight o'clock, and we prepared ourselves for a long, dry day. Mungai, who has incredible eyes, never took his eyes off the face of the hill. Because I had given my binoculars to Rikita I was forced to use my 400 mm telephoto lens to range the hill from left to right, west to east. I was sure the best chance of seeing the black leopard was against the brown dried grass. We didn't say much, realising that it was probably a futile plan. But I was hopeful. Gambles sometimes work, and I had gambled before.

It was a tiring and often boring experience, looking for a black dot on a brown hillside, and five hours later we were still there. No sign of a leopard, and no sign of Rikita or Alfred either. And then we saw another Land Rover coursing its way across the river making its way towards our hillock. At first I cursed it for disturbing our vigil, but then realised it was Will Craig bringing us some much-needed supplies of water and food. Will, although admiring our stamina, made no bones about the uselessness of our quest.

An hour after Will's departure Rikita appeared on the rise of our hillock. Approaching us he held out his hand. On it there was a single black hair. It could have been from any animal, and I suggested a zebra. But Rikita said that this was impossible; zebras are far too lazy to climb up Cave Hill and would always remain on the plains. Rikita was convinced that it was the hair of a leopard and that we should continue our watch. I was not so sure, but I was willing to continue with our plan. I searched the hill through my camera lens with renewed enthusiasm.

Three hours later we were still there. It was four o'clock and the heat was ebbing a little from the day. And then Rikita appeared again on the rise below us, hurrying. He spoke quickly to Mungai in Swahili and pointed to the back of Cave Hill. He claimed he had seen something moving in the long grass and that it might be a leopard. He wasn't sure, but if it were a leopard then it might take advantage of the coolness to move out of the shade and protection of the grass to a higher position on the hill. Mungai continued to scan the face of the hill. He was motionless, his eyes trained towards the eastern base of Cave Hill, towards the river, and above the long dry brown grass of the plains. Suddenly he quietly said to me:

"Quick, quick. There, the leopard, moving. Get your camera. Take the glasses. Look – above the acacia tree – to the left. Do you see it? You'll have to wait. I'll tell you when it moves. There. Now."

And then I saw it, just as Rikita had said, a small and indistinct black shape moving slowly across the face of Cave Hill. Up the hill diagonally, and then out of sight again behind long grass.

"Okay," Mungai said. "You stay with Christopher; I'll go and get Alfred. Don't lose sight of the leopard. It's getting dark, so you'll have to keep your eyes on him."

And then Mungai drove off, returning with an exhausted, parched Alfred a few minutes later. Rikita didn't take his eyes off the place where the leopard was crouching. Neither did I. And then we all saw the leopard again, looking at us across the divide between our hillock and Cave Hill. He lifted his black head above the grass and then lowered it again. Furtive. Cautious. A regulation tawny leopard would have been quite invisible in the light brown tones of the scorched hill grass. But this was a black leopard, an amazing sight . . . an extraordinary sight. We watched the cat for almost ten minutes, but there was not enough light to take any decent photographs. And then the sky became dimmer still, and it was almost evening. The African animal world was coming to life. Another world was starting.

⋆　⋆　⋆

We had no proof that we had seen the leopard, and although Will Craig believed us when we told him of our sighting, we knew that we needed to get cleaner photographs of the black leopard. And so at five o'clock the following morning Mungai woke me again. But this time he had brought with him a Maasai elder, and old man called Taraiyo from the Ilng'uesi reserve, who worked for the Craig family on the Lewa Ranch. Mungai told me that Taraiyo wanted to talk to me and wanted to come with us that day to search for the leopard. I agreed.

While gathering myself together, drinking strong coffee, packing my cameras, Taraiyo asked me over and over again, did you see the leopard? A black leopard? Are you sure? Is Mungai sure? I was certain and told him so, but the news seemed somehow to upset Taraiyo. He grew silent and thoughtful as we piled our gear into the Land Rover. He squeezed in the back with Rikita and Alfred. As we made our way in the darkness to the foot of Cave Hill Taraiyo leant over my shoulder and said, "If you saw the black leopard yesterday that is bad." I looked around at him. He was serious.

"Why?" I asked. Taraiyo didn't answer, but it was clear that he and Mungai had discussed the previous day's events. Rikita and Alfred were silent. Twenty minutes later we crossed the Lewa River and wound our way across the plains to the foot of Cave Hill. It was still dark when we stopped at the base of the hillock overlooking Cave Hill, but I got my cameras ready, as well as my video camera-recorder, and put them on the dashboard in front of me. We waited in silence, Mungai and I sitting, but the three Maasai standing in the back of the Land Rover. We waited, looking out on to the face of Cave Hill, where the sun's first rays would hit as dawn broke.

Suddenly both Rikita and Alfred shouted "*Chui*. There's the leopard."

Usually encountered in the dense tropical rainforests of southeast Asia, the melanistic leopard's dark colouration gives it better camouflage, where there is little sunlight.

"Where?" I shouted, standing up suddenly and grabbing my video camera. I looked out on to Cave Hill. "No, not there – there," Rikita yelled excitedly. And there on a small plain not fifty metres from the Land Rover, towards the base of Cave Hill, was the cat. I pressed the Sony camera into action, with fully extended telephoto lens. I kept filming while Mungai started the engine and very slowly drove towards the large, obviously male, black leopard. We guessed he had been down to the river to quench his thirst, but now he had seen us and scurried away, but not far. I kept filming whether or not the leopard was in the frame, even though I sometimes couldn't see him. He kept moving, and I kept filming. No one said anything. And then we lost him. I must have got about three minutes of the black leopard on film.

Taraiyo, who had been completely silent for some time, said, "Up there in the caves." We looked up the hill and saw the leopard again, and I got perhaps another minute of the leopard on film, further away but still clearly visible. It was lighter now, and the leopard made its way up the side of the escarpment, up the hill towards the caves where it obviously planned to spend the day out of the glaring sun. We waited another half-an-hour, but didn't see the beast again. I replayed the footage I had just taken. It was all there. Some of it was poor and badly shaken, particularly the footage I shot while the Land Rover was moving. But it was definitely there, thank God. At least three minutes of black leopard on film. In the excitement I had completely forgotten to take any still photographs.

"What do you want to do now?" Mungai asked me.

The day was starting to get hot and the leopard would not show itself again until the late afternoon and so there was no point in staying. There was a chance he would venture onto the plains to hunt, but this would not happen until much later, and so we decided to go back to the ranch for breakfast, all four of us together with Taraiyo. None of the others had ever seen a black leopard before, and Taraiyo certainly hadn't, even in his long seventy-year life. He was the only one who wasn't particularly happy. This made me anxious to talk to the Maasai elder, as I was sure that he knew something that he wasn't telling me. I was sure that his silence over the black leopard held a dark mystery, a riddle. I arranged to meet him later in the morning, but first I wanted to show the footage of the black leopard to Will Craig, who watched it in amazement, lost for words.

⋆   ⋆   ⋆

Taraiyo spoke English haltingly, always searching for the right words, understanding more than he could speak. He had a keen sense of history and a proud knowledge of legend and ritual. He was also an incredibly superstitious man, and he didn't like it that we had seen a black leopard, and far less that he too had seen the rare and mythological beast.

I met Taraiyo in a room next to the Lewa stables. He was a serious man, and I did not think that I could broach the subject of the black leopard straight away, so I decided to try to learn something of the Maasai, their traditions and ways. The Maasai are the most pastoral people of Africa and have not until very recently had laws on agricultural land. They speak the Maa language and seem always to have been divided into two groups: the agricultural people such as the Wa-Arusha in Northern Tanzania and the Baraguyu, whose economic life is agricultural and who contravene usual Maasai taboos. Outside this group are the tribes who live in northeastern Kenya, and among these are the Ilng'uesi of whom Taraiyo is a member. And even though today agriculture is practised, his Maasai people prefer a pastoral life, keeping cattle and moving across the plains of Africa moving to new grazing lands with the seasons. There is a common origin within the Maasai even though their lands have been isolated geographically by the process of colonization and the conversion of traditional Maasai lands into game reserves and national parks. Tall, elegant and handsome, the noble race has always seemed proud and totally indifferent to everything except the most pressing external influences.

The pre-colonial history of the Maasai is shrouded in myth. It is believed that they originated in a crater-like country surrounded by steep escarpments, which they left after a prolonged period of drought forced certain sections of the Maasai tribe to move away. They succeeded in conquering the escarpment and found themselves in the highlands of Kenya, where they live to this day. Their original dispersion area was almost certainly the northwestern shore of Lake Rudolph (now Lake Turkana in Northern Kenya). Then some time during the advent of British colonialism they trekked southwards to the Kerio Valley escarpment in Kalenjin country, before arriving in Laikipia and Wausinu Gishu in the Kenya Highlands. The Europeans checked further southward expansion, but not before the Maasai had reached the northern region of Tanzania. The Maasai also acted as a barrier between the Kenya and Uganda interior against the Arab slavers. Highways of commerce had to be secured during colonial times between Buganda and the coast. The shortest route to Lake Victoria lay through Maasai land. It was important because Buganda lay at the base of the Nile, and the Nile Valley strategy demanded control of the river by those who wanted to control Egypt and, through Egypt, the Suez Canal – the shortest gateway to the economic wealth of India and the East. It was for these reasons that Livingstone, Stanley, Burton, Speke, Grant and the Bakers were sent out. Adventure and geography were secondary considerations to economy.

Taraiyo seemed to welcome my understanding of Maasai history and particularly to agree that their power and wealth had been curtailed very much when the Europeans arrived in Africa. But, he said that despite the pressure on the Maasai to curtail their pastoral activities, the tribe itself retained its beliefs and traditions.

"We are not really Africans," Taraiyo continued. "We come from the Nile near the lands that used to be called Abyssinia and which is now called Ethiopia. We were not meant to stay in one place like now, growing vegetables and digging the earth. We are warriors and herdsmen. We are what you call nomads, following the rain and the new grass to feed our herds. This is important to us. This is our wealth. We kill anyone who stops our freedom. But now there are new laws. We cannot move from one area to another. After the white men came there are government and rules and laws and schools and roads. We must go where we are told to go – even though this is our land. They have taken away our land and taken away our freedom. And now they teach us the white man's way in the schools where we have to send our children. If you stop our freedom we will die. We cannot be prisoners and we cannot use our hands for labour work. We are warriors . . ."

There was a pause and I decided to risk all and ask him the question I'd been dying to ask. "But what about the black leopard? Why are you so worried that we have seen one of the rarest animals in the world? This is a very lucky thing for us."

"No. No. No," Taraiyo replied in quite an agitated state. There was a pained look in his eyes. "It is not a lucky thing. It is very unlucky and very bad. Always there are problems for us. First there are good rains and then more children, but always after that there will be no rain and drought and bad times. This is always the way when we see the panther, what you call the black leopard. It is evil and should be killed. If you do not kill it and use the oil from the body to rub on the children then they will be sick. Always this is the way. We must pray to Maa. He is the God that sees these things. He is looking now. We must give the black animal to him. God does not eat mankind. Evil cannot be contained. Darkness has ears, and you will soon understand that he who has a sharp mouth conquers the world."

I was amazed, and said nothing for a while. Taraiyo looked at his feet as if embarrassed by what he had said, as if he was talking about something that should not be mentioned to an outsider. These beliefs, he seemed to say, should only be discussed among the elders.

And then we were silent for a long time, Taraiyo continuing to look at the ground. He seemed uneasy and we both knew our short talk was ending. There was nothing else to say. I invited Taraiyo to come with us that afternoon, but was not surprised when he declined politely, saying he must return to Ilng'uesi and his people, as there was no more work for him at Lewa Ranch. We slowly walked out into the African sunlight together; two people from different worlds going our own separate ways.

☆   ☆   ☆

"Where shall we go?" Mungai asked me as Rikita, Alfred and I climbed into the old Land Rover later that afternoon.

"To the plains between the river and Cave Hill," I replied without much hesitation.

"Do you think it's too early?" It was only half past three and the sun was high in the sky. It was far too hot for predators to start out on their evening activities.

"It'll take us about half an hour to get there," Mungai replied. "If the leopard wants to hunt he'll have to come down to the plains before it gets dark."

And so we made our way out, away from the ranch, through the scrub jungle, across the Lewa River, and into the long dried grass plains below Cave Hill. On the left of the track a few impala grazed nonchalantly between the track and the river. A little further away some Burchell's zebra lazily rolled in some dust. Mount Kenya in the distance was only a blurry image clouded with the African haze. I filmed a Ruppel's vulture circling over the plains and a pair of ostrich females flapping their short wings over their backs. Mungai seemed in a sort of daydream and so was Alfred. There was no sign of the leopard.

At the foot of Cave Hill a lone thorn acacia was obscuring part of our view of the hill face, and I had thought of asking Mungai to move the Land Rover further along the track to the base of the hill. But it was still too hot, so I simply focused on the hill and the shallow ditch at the foot of it. And then I looked over and into the branches of the acacia tree. I saw a very slight movement – a stick hanging down from the shadows

My heart leapt. For there on the low right hand branch of the tree, with its black tail hanging down, was the black leopard looking at us. Straight at us.

under the tree about three or four metres above the found. What was it? Only a twig, but I kept my eyes on it. Could it be? I kept looking at it. And then it moved again – only a slight sway. Could it possibly be the leopard's tail? The tree was certainly an ideal platform for a leopard to prospect its territory.

"Mungai," I said, "take these glasses and have a look. Don't move. Don't anybody move." We were all sitting down.

"Where?" Mungai asked.

"Just to the right of the main trunk of the tree, on the right hand branch. Can you see something hanging down perpendicular? About four feet to the right of the trunk, below the first branch up from the ground. Do you see it? What do you think?"

"I can't see definitely," Mungai said. "We're too far away. Keep your small camera on the branch and I'll move the Land Rover closer."

"Don't move or stand up," I said. "Okay, Mungai. Go towards the tree, very slowly, really slowly. Not too far. Maybe about twenty or thirty yards." And as we moved closer, the shadows above the low branches of the acacia grew a little less dark.

"Stop," I said. "Give me the glasses." And then my heart leapt. For there on the low right-hand branch of the tree, with its black tail hanging down, was the black leopard looking at us. Straight at us.

"Here, Mungai. Take the glasses. Keep looking at the leopard. Tell me if he moves." With that I focused the video camera directly on the creature, which was still quite far away. We had already switched the engine off. I filmed the leopard looking at us from the shadows of the branching acacia for about a minute, but then he got up onto the branches.

"Damn," I said. "We've disturbed it. We've come too close."

I still had my camera on the leopard, which slowly crept down the jutting limbs of the tree and silently leapt down off the branch into the long brown grass below. We sat motionless for about five minutes, and then I said, "Mungai. Drive up to the tree slowly. Maybe he's on the ground in the grass and we'll see him move towards the hill."

Very slowly we went forward until we were almost under the tree. But still we saw nothing. And then I did a very stupid and dangerous thing. Desperate to get more footage of the black leopard, I got out of the Land Rover, slid myself into the long grass and strode slowly towards the tree. I told Mungai to stay with the vehicle, and told Alfred and Rikita to fan out either side of the tree about twenty metres away from where we had last seen the leopard. Then I waited until Alfred and Rikita were in place to the left and right of the tree and only a few paces from the base of Cave Hill. I kept my camera on in case something moved, not really caring about danger and what a cornered leopard might do. I had reached the base of the tree in a few minutes and had not seen anything. I waited patiently. Surely he must be here. I looked back. Mungai was glancing at us anxiously. And then I quietly told Alfred to move towards Rikita on the other side of the tree.

"Just move slowly," I said. Alfred moved.

He had only taken about four steps when he pointed in front of him and said, "The leopard is here. He is going to go up the hill."

I couldn't see anything but I moved quickly forward, the camera still filming, trained in the direction Alfred was pointing. He was standing still. And then I saw the leopard again, moving slowly, carefully, picking his way up the bank which was the base of Cave Hill, picking his way between the low scrub bushes, carefully, his long black tail behind him, his large black head low to the ground. The sun was darting on his shiny black back, just allowing us to see the faint rosettes on his body as he moved purposefully away from us. I kept the camera on, never once looking up. And then in less than thirty seconds it was all over. The leopard disappeared into some thick grass further up the hill, towards the escarpment below the caves. I turned my camera off, looked towards Alfred and Rikita and smiled. When I looked down at my boots and trousers I saw that my feet were covered in ticks. No one ever saw the black leopard again.

★　★　★

I left Kenya and Africa at the end of that week at Lewa Downs with the superstitious warnings of Taraiyo still taking up a great part of my mind. I had at long last seen a black leopard, but at what cost? I went out of my way to keep track of geophysical conditions and happenings in Northern Kenya. Then in August 2000, the year following our sighting of the black leopard, the Food and Agriculture Organization (FAO) in Kenya issued the following report:

> *Prospects for the 2000 main 'long rains' cereal crop, to be harvested from October in the main growing areas, are unfavourable. The long rains cropping season (March – May), which normally accounts for 80 per cent of total annual food production, has failed due to a severe drought. With the exception of parts of Western Province and Nyanza Province, the rest of the country, including the 'bread basket' Rift Valley Province, have received little or no rainfall, leading to widespread crop failures as well as large livestock losses in the pastoral areas of the north, north-east and north-west. Current official forecasts put the 2000 long rains maize crop at only 1.4 million tonnes, 36 per cent lower than the long rains average of 2.21 million tonnes and 22 per cent less that the drought-reduced 1999 long rains crop of 1.8 million tonnes. Assuming the 2000 short rains (October – December) harvest at the same level as in 1999, estimated at 450,000 tonnes, total domestic production available for consumption in 2000/01 amounts to 1.85 million tonnes. Maize stocks are estimated to be depleted at all levels throughout the country. With a national maize utilisation requirement (including food, feed, seed, losses) estimated at 3.21 million tonnes, Kenya will need to import some 1.4 million tonnes until the main harvest in September 2001.*

The country's food supply situation gives cause for serious concern with nearly 3.3 million people now estimated to be in need of urgent food assistance. Pastoralists are of particular concern as they are faced with the fourth consecutive failure of the rainy season. The current drought has aggravated an already severe scarcity of water and pasture and resulted in large livestock losses. Starvation-related deaths, particularly among children, are being reported. An Emergency Operation for US$88.5 million was jointly approved by FAO and World Food Programme (WFP) on 30 June 2000 to assist some 3.3 million people for a period of six months. Earlier in May, the Government appealed for international food assistance amounting to US$134.2 million, reflecting the large numbers of people faced with severe food shortages. The long drought has also drained reservoirs in dams, prompting the Government to take measures of rationing power for the next six months.

At the same time a rainfall chart was issued from Borana, an area adjacent to Lewa, where the 3.68 inches recorded in 2000 was almost the lowest recorded rainfall in 17 years. Swarms of locusts had further ravaged and depleted the arid grasslands and meagre crops, causing hardship and hunger. As Taraiyo had predicted, there had indeed been very bad times in the area for almost the entire year. Finding no work in Lewa, Taraiyo had eventually returned to Ilng'uesi. The small Maasai community still survives and now, seven years later, I often wonder what has become of Taraiyo, and whether the story of his extraordinary sighting of the black leopard is ever passed down to the children of this small but proud warrior community.

CHAPTER 9

The Semliki Leopard

CHRISTOPHER ONDAATJE

Since the mid-19th century, the discovery of the source of the Nile has been controversial. British explorers Richard Burton's and John Hanning Speke's legendary search ended after Speke claimed in 1859 to have discovered the Nile's source in the lake he named after Queen Victoria. Burton, who for enigmatic reasons, refused to journey from Tabora with Speke on this short northbound journey, rejected Speke's claim as being out of hand. Speke made a second journey with James Augustus Grant to Lake Victoria in 1860, finding the effluent of the lake at Rippon Falls. Samuel Baker and his wife Florence met Speke at Gondokoro, after which they made an intrepid journey to find Lake Albert.

In November 1996, nearing the end of a three-month journey tracing the footsteps of the Victorian explorers, I had reached Kasese at the foot of the Ruwenzori Mountains in Uganda. My quest was to unravel the mystery of the Nile's source – incorrectly designated by John Hanning Speke in 1858 as Lake Victoria. Far from being the source, Lake Victoria is in fact one of the two great reservoirs of the Nile – the other being Lake Albert – and they are fed by two mighty rivers: the Kagera, which drains the Burundi highlands, and the Semliki which drains the Ruwenzori Mountains. I had travelled from Zanzibar to Bagamayo on the east coast of Africa, and then to Tabora, Ujiji on Lake Tanganyika, Lake Victoria to Ripon Falls, down the Victoria Nile to Murchison Falls and the north end of Lake Albert, and eventually along the east coast of Lake Albert to Fort Portal and Kasese – a sleepy mountain village in the Ruwenzoris. My three travelling companions and I spent that night in the Margharita Hotel. Kasese is the usual base for expeditions up the Ruwenzoris. It is the westernmost terminus of the Uganda Railway and was once an important centre for the export of copper and cobalt mined at nearby Kilembe. However, the mines are no longer in operation. In Idi Amin's time, visitors were required to register with the police when they arrived and even submit all their currency for scrutiny. Hotels were regularly raided then, too, and the tourists detained for minor transgressions. Things are now more relaxed but, because of the refugee situation, which we were soon to witness in a very dramatic way, Kasese is still a dangerous town.

Exhausted, thirsty, and extremely hungry, we relaxed over some Nile beer before dinner. Dinner was a very hot goat curry – too hot. We discussed the Ruwenzori Mountains at length. Our initial plan was to spend six to eight days climbing some of the eastern slopes. I hoped to get at least above the cloud line to see the major peaks, and then view and make whatever conclusions I could about the drainage system from that elevated position.

The Ruwenzori Mountains extend for one hundred kilometres along the border between Uganda and Zaire (now the Republic of Congo). The local name is *Gambalagala*, 'my eyes smart', referring to the dazzling effect of the glaciers. The highest snow-covered peaks are Margharita at 5,119 metres on Mt. Stanley, followed by the peaks of Mt. Speke, Mt. Baker, Mt. Gessi, Mt. Emin, and Mt. Luigi di Savoia. We had been warned that the mountains were always extremely wet and cold.

The next day Kasese was in semi-chaos. Rebels – possibly from Zaire – had crossed over the border only ten kilometres west of the town and were moving down the Kazinga Channel, which runs between Lake

George and Lake Edward. The previously deserted streets of the town were now suddenly crowded with Ugandans fleeing their villages along the border with Zaire. We saw guns everywhere. In small groups, people were being herded first to one part of the town, then to another. Families sat on doorsteps along the narrow main street, guarding their meagre possessions. There were armed men everywhere, some in uniform, but many not. It was difficult to tell who was in charge. Even without understanding a word of the language we could tell that conversations were tinged with alarm.

We had wanted to start up the mountains as early as possible, but we had to wait until 9.00 a.m. when the Mountain Services offices opened. We asked about the possibility of hiking into the rainy highlands, and also about the drainage from the mountains into the Mbuku and the Rwimi rivers. Both of these flow eastward, while on the west side of the Ruwenzori range the Butawu, the Lunsilubi, the Rualoni, and the Lamya rivers flow into the Semliki River. We wanted to see for ourselves that the Semliki drained out of Lake Edward into Lake Albert, and also that the east-flowing rivers drained into Lake George and then into Lake Edward.

As we discussed our plans I began to change my mind about the course of action. Even though the visibility was terrible and conditions miserably wet and cold, it would still have been a great experience to climb the mountains. However, I felt that the six to eight days it would take to get high enough to see the peaks would be a poor use of our time. I was beginning to get a gut feeling that we should take a different tack. The journey down the east side of Lake Albert, up to Fort Portal and the Ruwenzoris, and then along the high escarpment had told me that there was more to the story than the mountains. I began to suspect that the answer to the riddle of the Nile lay in the deep valley on the western side of the Ruwenzori Mountains.

And so it was that I made my decision to round the southernmost tip of the Ruwenzori range until I reached the Semliki River on the Zaire border. Few people ventured into the region. We would be almost totally alone, or so we thought. As we were soon to find out, we would be in equatorial forest: dense, muggy, luxuriant, mosquito and fly-infested swamp land.

By the time we had packed and were ready to leave, Kasese was in complete turmoil, thronged with refugees from the border towns of both Zaire and Uganda. It took us nearly two hours to inch our way along the main street of Kasese, but we knew that it was in our best interests to be patient. There was no gunfire, which seemed quite amazing, considering the number of guns clearly visible and the high levels of tension. The morning we left there were more than five thousand people there. Quite obviously the town was not big enough to hold this crowd. Months later, watching the news on television in England, I saw the decimation of huge refugee camps that had grown up on the outskirts of Kasese. The camps must have been created soon after we were there, to provide shelter for thousands and thousands of homeless people: Zaireans, fleeing the conflict between Mbutu's forces and Kabila's tribal people from the Ruwenzori mountain slopes and from the border villages, Hutus from Rwanda and from the refugee camps in Zaire. Aggression followed the mass movement of people into Kasese. The television clip I later saw told the awful story. The area through which we had travelled became a gruesome scene of carnage, with thousands slaughtered – or uprooted again and forced to move on. Clearly while we were there, the area was not yet the powder keg it later became. It was quite tense enough for my taste, however. After we left Kasese we were stopped several times at roadblocks and closely questioned. There were troops all over the place. In retrospect, I am amazed that we never ran into real trouble. We seemed to be living a charmed life.

From Kasese we headed first to Fort Portal, where we stocked up on provisions. Then we set out for the Semliki Valley, at the foot of the Ruwenzoris near the border of Zaire. We drove along a spectacular, winding mountain road, overhung by steep-sided cliffs, dropping at least 1,500 metres. We passed thatched houses clinging to the sides of the mountains and banana and cassava plantations isolated high above the world. The road sometimes curved agonisingly around hairpin bends. Once in a while there was a bit of a landslide. Rocks skittered behind us while goats grazed nonchalantly on the roadside grass. We saw Ankole cattle with their enormous horns. I glanced out of the window and caught a glimpse of Zaire to the west.

We descended from the cloudy, damp atmosphere. There were hot springs in the flood plains below us and steam rose glistening in the afternoon sun, a reminder of the volcanic activity that still occurs here from time to time. As we descended it grew much hotter and drier. We were making our way out of the clouds. The vegetation also changed dramatically, its lush, deep greens giving way to the paler greens of the arid savannah. Below us stretched a huge valley and we caught sight of the sun sparkling on a meandering ox-bowed river – the Semliki. Again I wondered why none of the early explorers had made this journey. If Samuel Baker had continued all the way around to the south end of Lake Albert and found the river, he might well have argued that the Semliki was the source of the Nile. Had he seen the Ruwenzoris he would certainly have claimed for himself, with some justification, a more significant place in the pantheon of British explorers. In the end, however, we had to wait for Stanley, with his exhaustive research and explanation, and his own claims of discovery.

As we descended into the Semliki Valley I noticed that the lower we got, the shorter the people at the side of the roads seemed to be. Deeper into the valley, we began to see people carrying spears, then people with bows and arrows, then men with long beards. Eventually, almost at the foot of the mountains, we found ourselves in equatorial jungle, very humid and hot and dense, with massive trees soaring to great heights. We were right at the edge of the Semliki Forest Park – a virtually untouched tropical lowland forest, separated from the Ituri Forest of Zaire only by the Semliki River. After we had introduced ourselves to the park staff we set up camp in a small clearing not fifty metres from the rugged mountain road. Heading farther south into the jungle we found a small group of Bamba and Bakonjo people, often referred to as pygmies. It was getting late however and we soon headed back to camp. We ate dinner and settled in for the night – I alone in a small plastic tent some way from Thad Petersen and our two bearers from Tanzania. They were housed in a larger tent another thirty metres away. The pygmy settlement was a good three kilometres away from us and the entrance to the Semliki Forest Park.

The clearing in which we had camped was about forty-five metres square and completely surrounded by tall cane grass. It was dark, very dark, and I was lying on an uncomfortable ground-sheet, being bitten by minute insects which I was later told were *bukukums*. The bites left awful welts – particularly around the eyes and ears. It was difficult sleeping but I eventually dozed off.

Suddenly, it couldn't have been as much as an hour or so later, there was the sound of gunfire and shouting on the mountain road. I lay motionless, a virtual prisoner in my tent, remembering the harrowing scene I had witnessed a few hours earlier in Kasese. Refugees. What I had not realised was that that very night followed the day on which Laurent Kabila's troops had made their successful first attempt to overthrow the dictatorship of Mbutu in Zaire. It was a terrifying experience, and I had no idea what to do. For a good hour I listened to the turmoil and then, during a quieter period, I silently unzipped the front flap of my tent and shone my torch into the long grass into either side of the narrow path that led away from the clearing. Imagine my surprise when, instead of rebels, I saw two bright orange eyes shining back at me from the edge of the clearing. From long experience I realised that the bright coloured eyes could only be that of a large cat – perhaps a leopard. I shone my torch

The light of my torch revealed the tawny hide and abstract rosettes of a young female leopard, with her long twitching tail, motionlessly staring at some unseen object or horizon along the clearing path.

again on the motionless figure still looking at me. Then, without moving, the stealthy predator turned away and looked instead down the narrow path and towards the noise and turbulence of the distraught crowd surging forward on the mountain road. The light of my torch revealed the tawny hide and abstract rosettes of a young female leopard, with her long twitching tail, motionlessly staring at some unseen object or horizon along the clearing path. I didn't move. However, I kept shining my torch on the beast. After a few moments, perhaps as long as a minute, the leopard turned slowly and moved away from the path towards the centre of the clearing and to a location I could not see to the left and behind my tent. I dared not move or make a sound, but slowly, silently crouched down again on my ground sheet and turned off the light of my torch. The sounds of the rebels continued into the night taking on a more distant danger. Eventually the sounds of the forest around me became more realistic and more immediate and my ears began to be more aware of the noises around me. The occasional rustle of the wind in the trees, cicadas, the drone of a persistent mosquito, and always the distant clamour of the fleeing refugees. I prayed then. I thought of all the good things I had done in my life, and all the bad and selfish things. I thought of my family in England and in America. How would they look after themselves? How would they know if anything happened to me? I made a deal with God too. If I ever got out of this situation alive I would devote a great part of my life to doing some good in the world – particularly in learning and international understanding. But would I ever get the chance? I felt as alone then as I had ever been in my life and longed for some companionship. And then I became aware of another being's breathing. This time it was right next to my tent. I listened harder and there could be no mistake – a deep guttural breathing which could only be a few feet away. Had the dangerous cat sought protection or cover from my tent? Or had she indeed, aware of the dangers fifty metres away, looked to me for some sort of safety? It was hard to believe. Yet the situation, strange as it might appear, did exist. I tried to shine my torch through the thin plastic of my tent on the creature lurking inches away – but to no avail. I listened again. Her relaxed breathing continued. I felt somehow that the two of us had some undetermined, unspoken bond. As if together we were less vulnerable, perhaps even something of a threat to any passer by.

Suddenly I heard the voices. Distant at first, but closer and closer. Two people were definitely walking along the path towards the clearing. The hushed voices were unmistakable. I dared not shine my torch for fear of giving away my position and being discovered. It was a dark night and there seemed little likelihood that they would see our tents. In fact it was far more likely that they would trip over the guy ropes holding the fragile shelter upright. The voices grew louder, closer, and more insistent. I thought of running – but it would be certain suicide. What if they were armed? And then of course there was also the presence of the leopard. Neither of us had moved. Then, just as the voices were almost upon us and the probability of being found became a real possibility, I heard the rasping warning snarl of the leopard – only inches away from my left side. Immediately the voices were silenced, and a second or so later I distinctly heard the hurried retreating footsteps of the two strangers as they ran away from us back along the path to the mountain road. No further words were spoken and I lay motionless on my groundsheet as I listened to the eerie sounds of the night against the unhurried breathing of my strange companion. I must have slept because when I awoke the thin shreds of light that heralded the dawn shone through the upper branches of the equatorial forest. The front flap of my tent was still open as I had left it in the night. I was still too frightened to move, but eventually, as the morning became lighter, and as the echoing greeting calls of the jungle birds became bolder, I furtively looked out of my tent towards where my night companion had lain. But there was nothing to be seen. Not even a scratch or claw mark on the small dusty coloured ant hill that must have provided an uneven resting place for the leopard. She had completely and silently vanished.

A few minutes later a concerned Thad Petersen yelled across our clearing, "Are you all right, Chris?" "Yes," I replied, "Did you hear the commotion on the road?" "Of course," Thad replied, "but they all seem to have gone now." Indeed, there seemed no one around any more. I suppose that the exodus across the border took place at night to escape detection. "I think it's fairly safe now," he added.

"Did you see the leopard?" I asked. "What leopard?" Thad inquired. "Oh! I thought I saw a leopard last night sometime before midnight when the commotion first started. But I may have been mistaken." My strange encounter would have been too difficult to explain. And probably even more difficult to believe. I never mentioned the experience again.

Later that morning, at about 9.00 a.m., after a scanty breakfast of toast, cheese and coffee (no-one said much) we struck out west in our Land Rovers, bumping our way through tall cane grass and past cocoa plantations, the first we had seen. We then left our two vehicles under some cover, as we were still somewhat nervous of the rebels, and set out on a five-kilometre trek though deep swamps, the water sometimes up to our waists. We trudged through marshes and strands of papyrus, forded streams, and eventually found ourselves crossing open fields. On the flood plain we came upon a small number of villages, encampments of people who, while not actually pygmies, were nevertheless relatively short in stature. Like the pygmies, these tribespeople still hunt with bows and arrows and blow-pipes and poisoned darts. All their settlements were in very lush, well cultivated areas.

We went through thick, luxuriant jungle, crossed a deep tributary by dug-out canoe, trekked through an acacia grove, and eventually reached the Semliki River. It was about fifty metres wide, turbulent, full of silt, and flowing north at a swift rate towards Lake Albert. I looked up towards the Ruwenzoris to the south, covered in cloud, an amazing mountain range with peaks rising to five thousand metres. From the valley it felt as though the great mountains began at your ankles and swooped up to the clouds. The Mountains of the Moon. In this spot Samuel Baker would surely have said, "This has to be the source of the Nile."

*   *   *

My journey to unravel the secrets of the Nile's source had been short, measured in months instead of years as it did for the Victorian explorers. In terms of distance travelled, however, we had done quite well. Our journey had covered a total of 10,024 kilometres – roughly equivalent to one-fourth of the earth's circumference at the equator – and one and a half times the length of the Nile. The closer I came to departure the more I felt that Africa will always be a mystery. The more one learns the more there is to learn. At one time I really thought that I could offer some wisdom about Africa's past, some insight into its present and future. But in the end I felt that Africa always had and always would ultimately provide its own answers. I'm sure too that the Nile, like my extraordinary and mystifying confrontation with the Semliki leopard, just when it seems to have revealed all of its mysteries, will suddenly find a way to puzzle us anew.

CHAPTER 10

The Black Panther of Sivanipalli

KENNETH ANDERSON

The thousands of readers who already know Kenneth Anderson's stories of adventure in pursuit of the man-eating beasts of the Indian jungle will know what to expect from The Black Panther of Sivanipalli *which is also the 1959 title of his third and probably his best book. Few can equal him in jungle lore, his knowledge of the ways of wild creatures, of the hunters and the hunted, and none can tell a better story, full of excitement and colour, and crammed with unusual information. The author, who has spent a lifetime in trying to understand the minds of jungle creatures, takes us into his confidence and explains the methods by which he has been able to rid the remoter inhabitants of India of some of their most terrible enemies.*

Sivanipalli has always been a favourite haunt of mine because of its proximity to Bangalore and the fact that it lends itself so conveniently to a weekend excursion or even a visit of a few hours on a moonlit night. All you have to do is to motor from Bangalore to Denkanikotta, a distance of forty-one miles, proceed another four miles by car, and then leave the car and walk along a footpath for five miles, which brings you to Sivanipalli. The hamlet itself stands at the edge of the Reserved Forest.

Nearly three miles to the west of this small hamlet the land drops for about three hundred feet, down to a stream running along the decline. To the south of the hamlet another stream flows from east to west, descending rapidly in a number of cascades to converge with the first stream that runs along the foot of the western valley. To the east of Sivanipalli hamlet the jungle stretches to a forest lodge, Gulhatti Bungalow, situated nearly five hundred feet up on a hillside. East of Gulhatti itself, and about four and a half miles away as the crow flies, is another forest bungalow at a place called Aiyur. Four miles north-east again is a Forestry Department shed located near a rocky hill named Kuchuvadi. This is a sandalwood area and the shed houses an ancient and huge pair of scales which are used for weighing the cut pieces of sandalwood as they are brought in from the jungle, before being despatched to the Forestry Department's godowns at the block head-quarters at Denkanikotta.

Northwards of Sivanipalli thick scrub jungle extends right up to and beyond the road, five miles away, where you had to leave the car before setting out for the hamlet on foot.

Sivanipalli itself consists of barely half-a-dozen thatched huts and is hardly big enough to be called even a hamlet. A considerably larger village named Salivaram is found three miles to the north, just a little more than half way along the footpath leading to the main road.

Fire lines of the Forestry Department surround Sivanipalli on all four sides, demarcating the commencement of the surrounding reserved forest at distances varying from half a mile to a mile from the hamlet. There is a waterhole almost at the point where two of these fire lines converge at the southeastern corner. The two streams that meet west of the village at the foot of the three hundred-foot drop wind on through heavy jungle in the direction of another larger village named Anchetty, about eight miles southwestward of Sivanipalli itself.

I have given this rather detailed description of the topography of the surrounding region to enable you to have in mind a picture of the area in which occurred the adventure I am about to relate.

It is an ideal locality for a panther's activities, with small rocky hills in all directions, scrub jungle, heavy forest and two streams – apart from the waterhole – to ensure a steady water supply not only for the panthers themselves, but for the game on which they prey. Because of this regular supply of water a fairly large herd of cattle is quartered at Sivanipalli, which is an added attraction, of course, so far as these felines are concerned!

As a result, quite a number of panthers are more or less in permanent residence around the area. That is the main reason why I was attracted to Sivanipalli the first day I visited it in 1929.

The jungle varies in type from the heavy bamboo that grows in the vicinity of the waterhole to thick forest on the southern and western sides, with much thinner jungle and scrub, interspersed with sandalwood trees, to the east and north.

The countryside itself is extremely beautiful, with a lovely view of hills stretching away to a hazy and serrated blue line on the western horizon. Banks of mist float up from the jungle early in the morning and completely hide the base of these hills, exposing their tops like rugged islands in a sea of fleecy wool. On a cloudy day the opposite effect is seen, for when storm clouds settle themselves along the tops of the hills, entirely hiding them from view, only the lower portions of their slopes are visible, giving the impression of almost flat country.

I have spent many a moonlit night 'ghooming' – derived from the Urdu verb 'ghoom', meaning 'to wander about' – the jungles around little Sivanipalli. They hold game of every description, with the exception of bison, in moderate numbers. There is always the chance of encountering an elephant, hearing the soughing moan of a tiger, the grating sawing of a panther, or the crash of an alarmed sambar as it flees at your approach while you wander about the moonlit forest. You will not be able to see them – except perhaps the elephant, for both species of carnivora, and the sambar as well, are far too cunning and have long ago seen or heard you coming.

You may stumble upon a bear digging vigorously in the ground for white ants or tuber roots, or sniffing and snuffling loudly as he ambles along. You will undoubtedly hear him, long before you see him as a black blob in the confused and hazy background of vegetation, looking grey and ghostly in the moonlight.

As far back as 1934, Sivanipalli sprang a surprise. A black panther had been seen drinking at the waterhole by a herdsman returning with his cattle from the forest where he had taken them for the day to graze. It was shortly after five o'clock in the evening, which is the usual time for the cattle to be driven back to the pens in the village to be kraaled for the night. It is the custom to drive them out in the mornings to the jungle for the day's grazing at about nine, or even later, and to bring them back fairly early in the evening, the apparently late exodus and early return being to allow time for the cows to be milked twice a day.

Thus it was only a little after five and still quite light when the herdsman saw this black panther standing beside a bush that grew close to the water's edge, calmly lapping from the pool. He swore that it was jet black and I had no reason to disbelieve him, for there seemed no real point in a deliberate lie. When the herd approached, the panther had gazed up at the cattle; but when the herdsman appeared amidst his beasts it just melted away into the undergrowth.

Now the black panther is not a separate or special species. It is simply an instance of melanism. A black cub sometimes, but very rarely, appears in a litter, the other cubs being of normal size and colour. Black panthers are said to occur more in the thick evergreen forests of Malaya, Burma, Assam and similar localities than around this district. They have also been seen and shot very occasionally in the Western Ghats of India. I have every reason to believe in the view that they prevail in these heavy evergreen forests, for then their dark colour would afford considerably better concealment. At the same time, as they are simple instances of melanism, they should occur anywhere and everywhere that panthers exist, regardless of the type of jungle prevailing. But such has most definitely not been my own experience. I have only seen one other black panther in its wild state, and that was when it leapt across the road on the ghat section between Pennagram and Muttur near the Cauvery River, at about six one evening. They are one of Nature's – or rather the jungle's – mysteries that has never been quite satisfactorily solved.

If you look closely at a black panther in a zoo, you will discover that the rosette markings of the normal panther are still visible through the black hair, although of course they cannot be seen very distinctly.

When the herdsman saw this black panther he came to the village and told the people all about it. A black panther had never before been seen or heard of in this area and his tale was generally disbelieved. Having seen the animal with his own eyes, of course, he had no doubts, although he sincerely believed that it had not been a normal or living animal he had laid eyes upon but Satan in just one of the numerous forms he often adopts in the jungle to frighten poor villagers like himself.

Some weeks passed and no one saw or heard of the black panther again. The herdsman's story was forgotten.

One day, some months later, in mid-afternoon, with the sun shining brightly overhead, another herd of cattle was taking its siesta, squatting with closed eyes or lazily munching the grass in the shade of neighbouring trees. The beasts lay in little groups of two to half-a-dozen. The two herdsmen had finished their midday meal of ragi balls and curry, which they had brought along with them tied up in a dirty piece of cloth, and were fast asleep, lying side by side in the shade of another tree.

It was indeed a peaceful scene, as from an azure sky the tropical sun sent down its fiery rays that were reflected from the earth in waves of shimmering heat. The herd of cattle was relaxed, drowsy and unwatchful when the black panther of Sivanipalli took his first toll.

Appearing unexpectedly, the panther fastened his fangs in the throat of a half-grown brown and white cow, but not before she had time to bellow with pain and leap to her feet, lifting her assailant off the ground with his teeth locked in her throat.

The cow's agonized cry awakened one of the sleeping herdsmen, who was astounded by what he saw. He awoke his companion to look upon the Devil himself in an unexpected black form, and they watched as the stricken cow dropped to earth to ebb out her life, kicking wildly. The black panther maintained his grip. Thus she died. The men had leapt to their feet.

Ordinarily, in the event of an attack by a panther on one of their cattle they would have pushed to its rescue, brandishing their staves and shouting at the tops of their voices, if not actually to save the life of the victim, at least to drive off the attacker before he could drag away the kill.

In this case neither of them found the nerve to do so. They just stood rooted to the spot and gazed in astonishment. As they did so, the panther released his hold on the throat of the dead cow and looked in their direction. Although he was some fifty yards away they could clearly see the crimson blood gushing from the cow's torn throat and dyeing the muzzle of the panther a deep scarlet against the black background of fur.

They turned tail and fled.

When the few villagers of Sivanipalli heard this account they were very reluctant to go out and bring back the carcase before it was wholly eaten. This they would most certainly have done had the killer been a normal panther, but the presence of this unheard-of black monstrosity completely unnerved them. They had been told of a panther described as being jet black by the herdsman who had first seen him at the waterhole. Being villagers themselves, they had allowed a wide margin for exaggeration in that case, but here were two more herdsmen, both saying the same thing. Could it be really true?

After that day, the black marauder began to exact a regular toll of animals from Sivanipalli. He was seen on several occasions, so that there was no more doubt in the minds of any of the villagers as to his actual existence and colour.

THE BLACK PANTHER OF SIVANIPALLI

When the people came to know of his presence in the jungle, forcibly brought home to them by these frequent attacks on their animals, even their usual lethargy and apathy was shaken and they became more and more careful. Eventually a stage was reached when the cattle were not driven out to graze beyond a radius of about a quarter of a mile from the village.

Finding that his food supply was being cut off, the black panther started to extend his field of operation. He killed and ate animals that belonged to herds coming from Anchetty to the south-west and from Gulhatti and Aiyur to the east. He even carried off a large donkey from Salivaram, which, as I have said, lay to the north of Sivanipalli and well outside of the forest reserve proper.

Just about this time I happened to pay a visit to Sivanipalli accompanied by a friend. We had gone there after lunch on a Sunday, intending to take an evening stroll in the forest and perhaps get a junglefowl, or a couple of green pigeon for the pot. The story of the advent and activities of the black panther greatly interested me. I had only once before seen one of its kind outside a zoo, and I was therefore determined to bag this specimen if possible.

I offered to pay the villagers the price of the next animal killed by this panther if they would leave it undisturbed and inform me. They must go by bus to the small town of Hosur Cattle Farm, which was the closest place to a telegraph office, where a message could be sent to me at Bangalore. I also asked them to spread the same information to all persons living at places where the panther had already struck. Finally, as a further incentive and attraction, I said that I would not only pay for the dead animal, but give a cash baksheesh of fifty rupees to him who carried out my instructions carefully.

Anticipating a call within the next few days I kept my portable charpoy-machan and other equipment ready at Bangalore to leave within a few minutes of receiving the telegram. But it was over a fortnight before that call eventually came. Moreover it arrived late! That is to say, it reached me just before four o'clock in the evening. I was on my way by four-fifteen, but it was about seven-fifteen and quite dark by the time I reached Sivanipalli.

I noticed that the telegram had been handed in at Hosur Cattle Farm at about one-thirty that afternoon, which was far too late, apart from the additional delay that had taken place at the Bangalore end because it had been classed as an ordinary message, instead of an express telegram, as I had specified.

There was a man named Rangaswamy living at Sivanipalli, who had assisted me as shikari on two or three previous occasions, and it was this man who had sent the telegram from Hosur Cattle Farm to say that the panther had made a kill at ten that very morning, shortly after the cattle had left the village for grazing. The herdsman in charge, who like the rest had been told of my offer to pay for the animal that had been killed, with a cash bonus as well, had very wisely not touched the carcase but had run back to Sivanipalli with the news which he had given to Rangaswamy, who in turn had made a great effort to reach Denkanikotta in time to catch the twelve-fifteen bus. This he had just managed to do, reaching the Hosur Cattle Farm telegraph office by one o'clock.

Commending Rangaswamy and the herdsman for their prompt action in sending me the news, I now had to decide between trying to stalk the panther on his kill with the aid of torchlight or waiting at Sivanipalli until the following evening to sit up for him. The former plan was a complete gamble as there was no certainty whatever that the panther would be on the kill, or anywhere near it, when I got there. At the same time I could not find any very convincing excuse to justify spending the next twenty-four hours cooped up in the hamlet doing nothing.

I enquired where the kill had taken place and was informed that it was hardly half a mile to the west of the village, where the land began its steep descent to the bed of the stream about three miles away. It seemed too temptingly close and this decided me to tell Rangaswamy and the herdsman that I would endeavour to bag the panther that very night while he was eating the kill, if they would lead me to a quarter of a mile from the spot and indicate the direction in which the kill lay. I felt I could trust my own sense of hearing and judgement to guide me from there on.

They were both against this plan and very strongly advocated waiting till the following evening, but I said that I would like to try it anyhow.

By the time all this talk was finished it was ten minutes to eight and there was no time to be lost, as the panther would probably be eating at that very moment. I clamped my three-cell, fixed-focus electric torch, which was painted black to render it inconspicuous, to my rifle and dropped three spare cells into my pocket, together with five spare rounds of ammunition. Four more rounds I loaded into the rifle, keeping three in the magazine and one in the breech. Although the .405 Winchester is designed to carry four rounds in the magazine and one 'up the spout', I always load one less in the magazine to prevent a jam, which may occur should the under-lever be worked very fast in reloading. Lastly, I changed the boots I had been wearing for a pair of light rubber-soled brown 'khed' shoes. These would to a great extent help me to tread lightly and soundlessly. I was wearing khaki pants and shirt at the time, and I changed into the black shirt I generally wear when sitting up in a machan.

Rangaswamy and the herdsman came along with me up to a dry rivulet. Then the latter told me that this rivulet ran almost directly westwards with just two bends in its course to the spot where the panther had killed. He said the dead cow had later been dragged about two hundred yards inside the jungle roughly northwards of the place where the rivulet completed the second bend.

Their instructions were clear enough and I was grateful for the two bends in the stream which enabled them to be so specific. Telling the men to go back, as I would eventually be able to find my own way to Sivanipalli, I started out on my attempt.

I considered the wisest and most silent approach would be along the bed of this dry stream rather than along the top of either of its banks. Any slight sounds I might inadvertently make would then be muffled and less audible to the panther. Secondly, by walking along the bed of the stream I could easily follow its course without having to shine my torch to see where I was going, which I might have to do if I were to walk along the bank where the vegetation would impede me, the more so because it was very dark indeed and the sky very overcast, the clouds completely hiding the stars and whatever pale light they might have cast.

Accordingly I moved forward very carefully and soon felt the stream making its first curve, which was in a southwesterly direction. After a while the stream started to turn northwards again, and then straightened out to resume its westerly course. I had passed the first of the two bends the herdsman had mentioned.

Not long afterwards it curved into its second bend, but this time in a northerly direction. I moved as carefully as possible to avoid tripping upon any loose stone or boulder that might make a noise. Although, from the information I had been given, I knew the kill was still about three hundred yards away, panthers have very acute hearing, and if my quarry were anywhere in the immediate vicinity, if not actually eating on the kill, he would hear me and, as like as not, make off again.

Fortunately the rivulet was more or less clear of boulders and bushes along this part of its course and this helped me to edge along silently. A little later it had completed its northward turn and it began to curve southwards. After a few yards it straightened out once more and resumed its main westerly direction.

I halted. I had reached the place at which the panther had killed the cow and from where he had dragged the kill into the jungle for about two hundred yards to the north. I knew that I must now leave the rivulet and strike off into the undergrowth to try and locate the carcase and the killer, whom I hoped to surprise in the act of eating. In the deep gloom I had only my sense of hearing to guide me.

I tiptoed towards the northern bank of the stream which was, at that spot, only breast-high. With my feet still on the sandy bed, I gently laid the rifle on the bank and, folding my arms across my chest, I leaned against it, listening intently.

Five minutes passed, but there was no sound of any kind to disturb the silence. Perhaps the kill was too far away to allow me to hear the panther eating; that is, if he was on the kill and if he was eating.

Putting my weight on my hands, I gently drew myself up to the top of the bank, making no sound as I did so. I then picked up the rifle and started to move forward very, very slowly. The darkness was intense. At the same time I knew I had really little, if anything, to fear from the panther should he discover me, as he was not a man-eater and had shown no inclination at any time to molest human beings. Nevertheless, this was my first experience with a black panther and I had heard several of the usual stories about them being exceptionally dangerous and aggressive. That made me quite nervous, I can honestly tell you.

Inching forward, I stopped every few yards to listen for sounds that would indicate that the panther was busy eating. Only they could guide me, as it was hopeless to expect to see anything without the aid of my torch, which could only be used when I was close enough to fire. The slightest flicker of the beam now would drive the panther away should he happen to see the light.

I went along in this fashion, taking what seemed an interminable time. Perhaps I had progressed seventy-five yards or more when, during one of the many stops I made to listen, I thought I heard a faint sound coming from in front and a little to the right. I listened again for some time, but it was not repeated.

Bushes and trees were now growing thickly around me, and my body, in pushing through the undergrowth, was making some noise in spite of the utmost care I was taking to prevent this. So were my feet as I put them down at each tread. I tried pushing them forward by just raising them off the ground and sliding them along, but I was still not altogether silent. I did this not only to try and eliminate noise, but to disguise my human

footfalls should the panther hear me. He would certainly not associate any sliding and slithering sounds with a human being, but ascribe them to some small nocturnal creature moving about in the grass and bushes; whereas the sound of an ordinary footfall would immediately convey the fact that there was a man in the vicinity. An uncomfortable thought came into my mind that I might tread on a poisonous snake in the dark, and the rubber shoes I was wearing did not protect my ankles. I dispelled that thought and tried walking around the bushes and shrubs that arose before me. This caused me to deviate to some extent from the northerly course towards the dead cow I had been instructed to follow.

I stopped every now and then to listen, but the sound I had last heard was not repeated. It was some time later that I concluded that I had far exceeded the distance of two hundred yards from the rivulet at which the kill was said to be lying, and also that I had hopelessly lost all sense of direction, enveloped as I was amongst the trees and scrub, under an overcast sky.

Then suddenly I heard the sound I had so long been hoping to hear – the unmistakable sound of tearing flesh and crunching bones.

I had been lucky indeed. The panther was on his kill at that moment and, what was more, was actually engrossed in feeding. Now all I had to do was to try to creep sufficiently close to enable me to switch on my torch and take a shot. But that was all very well in theory. The idea was far easier than its execution.

To begin with, the sounds did not come from the direction in which I was moving, but to my left and some distance behind me, indicating that I had not steered a straight course in the darkness. I had veered to the right, by-passing the kill. Perhaps the reason I had not heard the sound of feeding earlier was because the panther had only just returned.

Black panthers are said to occur in the thick evergreen forests of Malaya, Burma, Assam and similar localities . . . They have also been seen and shot very occasionally in the Western Ghats of India.

Or – and it was a most discomforting thought that came into my mind – maybe he had heard me in the darkness as I passed and deliberately stayed quiet.

I paused for a few moments and listened so as to make quite sure of the direction from which the sounds were coming. In the darkness I guessed the panther to be anything from fifty to a hundred yards away.

I now started to slide my feet forward very slowly and very cautiously towards the noise.

If the panther had dragged his kill into or behind a bush it would be impossible for me to get the shot I hoped for. On the other hand, all the advantages would be with the panther were I to fire and wound him, and if he attacked the proposition was altogether a most unpleasant one.

At the same time, I tried to encourage myself by remembering that this panther had never before molested a human being, and that the light from my torch, when eventually I flashed it, would fill him with fear and keep him from attacking me, if it did not drive the animal off entirely.

It is difficult to describe truthfully the minutes that ensued, or to recount what I actually did. My mind and senses were so alert and intense, that I negotiated all obstacles in the way of trees and under-growth automatically. I knew that as long as I could hear the sounds made by the panther as he feasted I could be certain that he was fully engaged on the task at hand and was unaware of my approach. It was only when these sounds ceased that I would have to look out, for then the panther had heard me and had stopped his feeding to listen.

The sounds continued and so did I, creeping forward cautiously, never putting my foot down till I had tested each step with my toe. When I heard or sensed a leaf rustle beneath me, I groped for a place where I could tread more silently. All the while I kept my eyes strained upon the darkness before me and my ears pricked for the sounds of feeding.

Then suddenly those sounds stopped, and an absolute, awful silence engulfed me.

Had the panther stopped eating for a while of his own accord? Had he finished and gone away? Was he just going away? Or had he heard my stealthy approach and was even at that moment preparing to attack? The alternatives raced through my mind and I came to a halt too.

I remained thus, silent and stationary, for some time. Just how long I have no idea, but I remember that I was thinking what I should do next. To move forward, now that he had stopped eating, would certainly betray my approach to the panther – that is, if he was not already aware of my presence. However careful I might be, it would be impossible for a human being to move silently enough in the darkness to be inaudible to the acute hearing of such an animal. On the other hand, if I stayed put and kept quiet, there was a chance that I might hear the panther, should he approach, although panthers are well known to move noiselessly.

Of the two courses of action, I decided on the latter, so I just stood still. As events were shortly to prove, it was lucky that I did so.

For a few moments later a very faint rustling came to my straining ears. It stopped and then began again. Something was moving in the darkness before me; but that something might have been anything. It was a continuous sort of noise, such as a snake would make as it slithered through the grass and undergrowth. But a panther could just as easily cause it by creeping towards me on his belly. I can assure you that it was a very frightening thought.

One thing was certain. The sound did not come from a rat or a frog, or some small jungle creature or night bird. Had such been the case, the faint noise would have been in fits and starts; in jerks, as it were, each time the creature moved. But this was a continuous sort of noise, a steady slithering or creeping forward, indicating slow but continuous progress. It was now certain beyond all doubt that the sound was being made by one of two things: a snake or the panther.

I have taken some time in trying to describe to you my innermost thoughts as they raced through my mind. In actual fact, they raced through so fast that I had made up my mind within a few seconds of hearing that ominous, stealthy, creeping approach.

Another few seconds longer and I had decided that the panther was certainly creeping towards me, but as long as I could hear him I knew I was safe from any attack. Then abruptly the noise ceased.

Next came the well known hissing sound, comparable with that made by an angry cobra when it exhales the air from its body in a sudden puff. The panther was beginning to snarl. Very shortly he would snarl audibly, probably growl, and then would come the charge. I had heard the same sequence of noises often enough before and knew what to expect. Quickly raising the rifle to my shoulder, I pressed the switch of the torch.

Two baleful reddish-white eyes stared back at me, but I could make out nothing of the animal itself till I remembered I was dealing with a black panther, which would be practically invisible at night.

Perhaps it had at first no vicious intentions in approaching me, but had just sneaked forward to investigate what it had heard moving about in the vicinity of its kill. But having identified the source as a hated human being, that hissing start to the snarl showed that the black panther had definitely decided to be aggressive. His eyes stared back at the light of my torch without wavering.

I had plenty of time in which to take careful aim. Then I fired.

Instead of collapsing as I hoped and expected, or at least biting and struggling in its death throes, the panther sprang away with a series of guttural roars. Had I missed entirely, or had I wounded the beast ?

I felt certain that I could not have missed, but that was a question that could only be settled by daylight. I turned to retrace my steps.

This time, of course, I was free to use my torch, and with its aid I walked back roughly in the direction I had come.

I had thought wrong, however, and floundered about for half an hour without being able to regain the rivulet up which I had approached.

I looked at the sky. It was still cloudy and I could not pick out a single star that would help set me, even roughly, in the right direction to Sivanapalli village. Then I remembered that the land sloped gently westwards from the hamlet towards the ravine formed by the two rivers to the west. Therefore, if I walked in a direction that led slightly uphill I could not go wrong and would surely come out somewhere near the village.

I started walking uphill.

But I did not reach Sivanipalli or anywhere near it. To cut a long story short, it was past eleven thirty that night when I landed, not at Sivanipalli or its precincts as I had expected, but more than halfway up the track leading northwards to Salivaram. After that, of course, I knew where I was and within half an hour had reached the village.

There I awoke Rangaswamy and related what had happened. There was nothing more to do then than bed down for the night.

I have told you already that Sivanipalli was a small place boasting scarcely half a dozen huts. Rangaswamy himself was a much-married man with a large household of women and children and I could not expect him to invite me into his hut. So I lay down in a hayrick that stood a little off the main path and pulled the straw, already damp with dew, over me to try and keep warm.

If you should ever wish to undergo the lively experience of being half-eaten alive by the tiny grass ticks that abound in and around forest areas in southern India, I would recommend you to spend a night in a hayrick at Sivanipalli. You will assuredly not be disappointed. The grass tick is a minute creature which is normally no larger than the head of a pin. After it has gorged itself on your blood it becomes considerably larger. But it is a most ungrateful feeder. Not only does it suck your blood, but it leaves a tiny wound which rapidly develops into a suppurating sore. This increases in size in direct proportion to the amount of scratching you do to appease the intolerable itch and eventually turns into quite a nasty sore with a brown crust-like scab, and a watery interior. Moreover, should many of these creatures favour you with their attention at the same time, you will surely get a fever in addition to the sores.

I hardly slept at all during the rest of that confounded night, but spent the remaining hours of darkness scratching myself all over. Dawn found me a very tired, a very disgruntled and a very sore individual, who had most certainly had the worst of that night's encounter with the enemy – in this case the almost microscopical little grass tick.

The first thing to do, obviously, was to make some hot tea to raise my morale, which was at a decidedly low ebb, and with this in view I went to Rangaswamy's hut, only to find the door closed fast. It was evident that the inmates intended making a late morning. This did not fit in with my plans at all, so I pounded on the solid wooden structure and called aloud repeatedly. After quite a time I heard sounds of movement from within. Eventually the wooden bar that fastened the door on the inside was withdrawn, and a very tousled-headed, sleepy Rangaswamy emerged.

I instructed him to light a fire, which he started to do on the opposite side of the village road by placing three stones on the ground at the three points of a triangle, and in the middle making a smoky fire with damp sticks and straw. I had not brought any receptacle with me for boiling water, so I had to borrow one of his household earthenware pots, which he assured me was absolutely clean, a statement which I myself was not quite prepared to believe from its appearance.

However, the water eventually boiled. I had put some tea leaves into my water bottle, after emptying it of its contents, poured in the boiling water, recorked it and shook it in lieu of stirring. In the meantime the inmates of the other huts had come to life. They watched me interestedly. Some offered a little milk, and someone else contributed some jaggery, or brown sugar, for which I was very grateful, having also forgotten to bring sugar. We boiled the milk and put some lumps of jaggery into my mug, adding tea and boiling milk. Believe it or not, it brewed a mixture that did have some resemblance to tea.

Breakfast consisted of some eggs which I purchased and hard boiled over the same fire. By about seven I had restored enough interest in myself and events, after my dreadful encounter of the previous night with those obnoxious little ticks, to think of doing something about the panther.

I asked Rangaswamy to get the herdsman who had accompanied us the previous night and who had not put in an appearance so far that morning, or one of his companions, to collect a herd of buffaloes if they were obtainable and drive them into the thick undergrowth to dislodge the panther, as I felt confident I had not missed the brute entirely with my one shot.

All present answered that there were no buffaloes in Sivanipalli, and no one was willing to risk his cattle being injured in a possible encounter with the panther. Just then my missing companion of the night before – the herdsman who had accompanied me – turned up. He said that he had a friend at Salivaram who owned a muzzle-loading gun. He had wanted to borrow the gun so as to come along and assist me, and with that in view he had set out to Salivaram early that morning while it was yet dark. Unfortunately, his friend was away with his gun and so he had been unable to borrow it. He had returned empty handed.

I thanked him for his thoughtful intention to assist me, but inwardly I am more than thankful that he had been unsuccessful in borrowing the muzzle-loader. With an inexperienced user, a muzzle-loader can become a mighty deadly weapon and I confess I would have felt most nervous with him and that gun behind me.

Having failed to obtain the use of buffaloes, I then tried to enlist the cooperation of the owners of such village curs as there were at Sivanipalli. After some humming and hawing, one solitary cur was produced. She was a lanky bitch, with ears cut off at their base, entirely brown in colour, with a tremendously long curved tail. The typical example of a village 'pariah dog', as they are called, whose ears had been amputated when a puppy because of the ticks which would in later life have become lodged on and inside them. With villagers, it is a simple process of reasoning to come to the conclusion that it takes less effort, and far less time, to cut off the ears of their dogs when they are puppies than periodically to remove scores of ticks in later life.

By a strange coincidence, this bitch was named 'Kush', which reminded me of the name of the dog 'Kush Kush Kariya' owned by my old friend of jungle days, Byra the Poojaree. I don't know if this name is a favourite among the dog owners of the forest areas of Salem District, or whether it just lends itself to a natural sound emitted to attract the attention of any dog. Personally I am inclined to the latter idea. Whatever it may be, I did not know then that this bitch Kush would conduct herself every bit as precociously as her namesake, the animal owned by Byra.

Finally, accompanied by Rangaswamy, the herdsman, Kush and her owner, we set off to try and find out what had become of the panther.

We retraced our steps of the night before to the spot where my companions had left me, then followed in my own footsteps along the two bends in the rivulet and finally climbed its northern bank at the place I had chosen the previous night.

Thereafter I led the way with cocked rifle, Kush running between me and her owner, who came last in file. Between us came Rangaswamy, with the herdsman behind him.

As I had already discovered the night before, the undergrowth was dense, so that there was no means of tracing the exact course I had followed only twelve hours previously; nor, being daylight, was I able to pick out any of the trees or bushes I had negotiated in the darkness, although I knew roughly the direction in which I had gone.

The herdsman, of course, knew where the kill lay, but I did not want to go directly to it, my idea being to find, if possible, the place where I had fired at the panther. I did not succeed. Those who have been in jungles will understand how very different in size, shape and location just a small bush appears in daylight compared with its appearance at night. Darkness greatly magnifies the size of objects in the forest, distorts their shape and misleads as regards direction.

To help me find what I was looking for, I got the herdsman to lead us to the dead cow, which he found without difficulty. Incidentally, it had been half-eaten, although of course there was no means of knowing just then whether the panther had fed before my encounter with it, or whether I had entirely missed him and he had returned to feed after I had left. Panthers sometimes return to their kill if they are missed, although such behaviour, in my experience at least, is not very common.

Having reached the kill, I now tried to recollect and recast the direction from which I had come, so as to try and follow my own footsteps from there and eventually come to the spot where I had fired. Unfortunately I had no means of knowing exactly how far the panther had crept towards me, but had to rely entirely on my own judgement as to how far away he had been when I first heard him feeding. Sounds in a jungle at night, when both the hearer and the origin of the sound are enveloped by the surrounding undergrowth, can be very deceptive, and the distance they may travel is hard to guess for that very reason. I felt that to the best of my knowledge, I could have been standing anything from fifteen to fifty yards from the dead cow.

Deciding approximately on the distance where I might have been standing, I paced off those fifteen yards and got one of the men to mark the spot by bending down a small branch. Then I paced another thirty-five yards to attain the maximum distance of fifty yards, which I judged would be about the greatest that could have separated me from the feeding panther I had heard the night before. Here we bent another branch.

Somewhere in between these two markers, and very approximately in the same direction as I was walking, I knew I should find some sign of whether my bullet had struck the panther. If I did not find anything then I would have to conclude that I had completely missed him.

By this time I was also sure that the panther, if he had been wounded, was not lurking anywhere in the immediate vicinity, for had that been the case he would undoubtedly have given some sign by now, hearing us walking about and talking. That sign would have been in the form of a growl, or perhaps even a sudden charge. The absence of any such reaction and the complete silence led me to conclude that even if I had hit him, the wound was not severe enough to prevent him from getting away from the spot.

I instructed my three companions to cast around in a circle, and search carefully for a possible blood trail. I joined them and it was not very long before Kush, sniffing at something, attracted her owner's attention. He called out that he had found what we were looking for. Gathering around him and the bitch we saw an elongated smear of dried blood on a blade of lemon grass.

My spirits rose considerably. Here was proof that I had not missed. The height of the blood mark from the ground indicated that I had wounded my quarry somewhere in the upper part of his body, and as I knew I had fired between his eyes as they had reflected my torchlight, my bullet must have grazed his head. Alternatively, if he had happened to be crouching down with raised hindquarters at that time (a rather unlikely position for a panther to adopt when creeping forward), my bullet might be embedded itself somewhere in the rear part of his back.

This was where Kush showed her merit. She was a totally untrained cur, but she instinctively appeared to sense what was required of her. For a little while she sniffed around wildly and at random, then started to whine and run ahead of us.

We followed and found more blood smears on leaves and blades of grass where the panther had passed. Between the bushes and clumps of high grass there were spots of blood on the ground too. This was an encouraging find, as it showed that the animal had been bleeding freely, clear evidence that the wound was not just a superficial graze.

The blood itself had mostly dried, except in some very sheltered places. There it was moist enough to be rubbed off by the fingers. However, it was neither thick nor dark enough to suggest that my bullet had penetrated a vital organ, such as a lung.

Kush set out very rapidly in a westerly direction, and it was quite obvious she was following a trail that would eventually bring us to the sharp decline in the land, down to the bed of the stream flowing from north to south before it joined the other stream lower down and turned westwards. This stream, before its confluence, is known as the Anekal Vanka. The combined streams are called Dodda Halla, which in the Kanarese language literally means the 'Big Gorge'. It has this name because so many sections flow through ravines and gorges as they twist and twine a torturous path past the village of Anchetty. There the river changes its course abruptly and turns southwards, past Gundalam, to its eventual junction with the Cauvery River. It is this same stream, the Dodda Halla, that was once the haunt of the man-eating tiger of Jowlagiri, but that is another story. I have explored every section of it, right up to the place where it joins the Cauvery, and have nicknamed it the 'Secret River', partly because of the fact that, due to the many miles of rough walking entailed in following its course, few people come that way, and it is delightfully lonely and far away from the sight and sound of human beings; also because I have discovered secrets of geological interest along its banks. I hesitate to divulge them, for with their publicity must automatically follow the next necessary evil, the violation of the sanctity of one of the most delightfully isolated jungle localities in Salem District.

Returning to events as they occurred that morning. The undergrowth was very dense, but to the unerring instinct of Kush this appeared to offer no obstacle. In fact, the trouble lay in keeping up with her. Her small and lithe brown body dodged in and out between bushes and outcrops of 'wait-a-bit' thorn. Our legs, hands and arms were severely lacerated by these thorns because we were moving at a foolish speed in order to keep the bitch in sight, taking no precautions whatever against a sudden attack by the wounded panther if he happened to lie immediately ahead of us. At times the brambles and other obstructions slowed us down, and Kush would get far ahead and disappear. It then became necessary to whistle her back, and when she did so, which was only after some minutes, she appeared to experience some difficulty in picking up the trail again.

We had no rope with us, so I borrowed the herdsman's turban and knotted one end of the cloth around Kush's neck, giving the other end to her owner. But it was a small turban and the cloth too short. The man had to stoop down to retain his hold, while Kush strained, spluttered and coughed in her anxiety to forge ahead.

In this fashion we progressed until we eventually reached the edge of the plateau where the land began to fall away sharply to the bed of the Anekal Vanka stream, which we could see between breaks in the tree-tops below us, the sun glinting on the silvery surface of the water as it meandered from side to side of its sandy bed. The stream itself was three-fourths dry at that time of the year.

A little later we came across the first concrete evidence that the panther had begun to feel the effects of his wounds. He had lain down in the grass at the foot of a babul tree and had even rolled with pain, as blood was to be seen in patches and smears where he had rested and tossed. Kush spent a long time at this spot and evinced another unusual characteristic by licking at the blood. Ordinarily a village cur is terrified of a panther, but Kush, as I have said already, was an unusual animal, and it was indeed very lucky that her owner had been willing to bring her along. Normally, villagers who will not hesitate to lop off the ears of a puppy at their base, will vote that it is a cruel practice to employ a dog for tracking down a wounded panther or tiger and will flatly refuse to be parties to such a deed. As it was, without the invaluable aid rendered by this bitch, we would never have been able to follow the blood trail as we did that morning. It would not have been visible to normal human eyesight in the heavy underbrush.

As we descended the deep decline vegetation became sparser and the ground became bare and rocky. Boulders were scattered everywhere, interspersed with tufts of the tough long-bladed lemon grass.

Then we reached a stage where there were only boulders, big and small, and the descent had almost ended. This was the high-level mark reached by the waters of the stream when in spate during the monsoon.

Here, with the end of the vegetation, tracking became easy. Drops of telltale rusty brown, where blood had fallen from the wounded animal and splashed on the rocks, revealed its passage. Judging from the distance we had come and the quantity of blood that the panther had lost, it appeared to be more severely hurt than I had at first imagined. The wound must have been a deep one and the bullet had probably struck an artery. Had it been elsewhere, particularly in some fleshy part of the animal, there was a possibility that the bleeding might have lessened, if not ceased entirely, by the natural fat under the skin coming together and closing the hole made by the bullet.

We reached the narrow bed of the stream in which the water was still flowing. Here the panther had crouched down to drink, and there were two sets of blood marks, one nearer to the water's edge than the other. The marks further away indicated more bleeding than those closer. This was curious and it puzzled me greatly at the time, considering I had fired only one shot the night before. The solution was an even greater surprise.

At one spot the panther had stepped into his own gore and had left a clear pug mark on a rock just before he had waded across the stream. The mark had been made by one of the animal's forefeet and its size suggested a panther of only average proportions that was probably male. The blood had been washed off the foot by the time the animal had reached the opposite bank, but the dried drops on the stones and boulders continued.

After crossing the stream the panther had changed his course and had walked parallel with the edge of the water and alongside it for nearly two hundred yards, then he had turned to the left and begun to climb the opposite incline. The stones and rocks once more gave way rapidly to vegetation, and again we negotiated thickets of long grass, thorny clumps, small scattered bamboos and trees.

Up and up the panther had climbed, and so now did Kush on the trail, conducting herself as if she had been specially trained for the job. Eventually we came to the road which leads from Denkanikotta to Anchetty and which intersects the forest on its way downwards to the latter village. We had come out on this road exactly opposite the 9th milestone, which we now saw confronting us at the roadside. Incidentally this was the road on which I had parked my car near the 5th milestone when I had left it the evening before to walk to Sivanipalli.

Many carts had traversed the road during the night and in the earlier hours of that morning, and the scent was completely lost for a moment in the powdery brown dust. But Kush had no difficulty in picking it up on the other side, and we followed behind her.

The grass and bamboos gradually gave way to more thorns and more lantana, which tore at our clothing and every part of our anatomy they touched. In places, where the panther had crept beneath the lantana and thorn bushes, an almost impenetrable barrier confronted us. There was no way through and there was no way around, leaving no alternative but to follow by creeping on our bellies beneath the bushes.

My rifle was an encumbrance in such places and conditions, and I cursed and swore as the thorns tore at my hair and face and became embedded in my hands, body and legs. The plight of my three companions was infinitely worse, as they wore thinner and less clothing than I did. Perhaps their skins were thicker – I really don't know. But I am sure that the language that floated from all four of us would have won us prizes in any Billingsgate contest. Only Kush was unperturbed, and from her position ahead she kept looking back at us, clearly impatient at the slow, clumsy progress we were making.

By this time it was also evident that the wounded animal was heading for a large hill that lay about half a mile behind a hamlet named Kundukottai. This village was situated between the 7th and 8th milestones on the Denkanikotta–Anchetty road which we had just crossed. The top of the hill was known to hold many caves, both large and small and, what was worse, the arched roofs of some of the larger caves had been chosen by the big jungle rock bees as safe and ideal places in which to construct their hives. I had often seen these hives as I had motored along the road to Anchetty on previous occasions.

I felt that my chances of bagging the black panther were becoming very dim indeed. Looking for him amongst those caves would be like searching for the proverbial needle in a haystack. In addition, the panther had the bees to guard him if his place of retreat happened to be one of the many caves they had chosen for their hives. I can assure you that these rock bees, when disturbed, can be most formidable opponents.

We plodded along and broke cover below the line of caves where the thorn bushes thinned out and became less numerous owing to shelves of sloping rock, worn glass smooth by centuries of rain water as it ran down from above.

The scent led up and across the sloping shelf of rock to one of the larger openings that loomed above us. From where we stood we could see the black masses of at least half a dozen beehives hanging from the roof of the cave, each about a yard long by about two feet wide. The remains of old abandoned hives were scattered here and there amongst them, the wax sticking out from the rock in flattish triangles of a dirty yellow-white colour, perhaps nine inches long.

My canvas-soled shoes enabled me to climb the slippery shelf without much difficulty, while the bare feet of my companions helped them even more. Kush's claws made a faint clicking sound as she scampered up the rock ahead of us.

We reached the entrance to the cave where a subdued rustling sound was all pervading. It came from the movements of millions of bees as they crawled in and about the hanging hives above us. There was also a continuous faint droning, that arose from the wings of the busy insects as they flew in from the jungle with honey from the wild flowers, which they would store in the hives, and from those departing on a trip for more.

The little creatures were absorbed in their duties and paid no attention to us, but we realized that if we happened to disturb them, these same little creatures, so unoffending and peaceful now, would pour on to us in a venomous attack like a torrent of black lava and sting us to death in a matter of a few minutes.

We stood before the entrance of the cave, where the blood trail, very slight now, was still visible in the form of two tiny dried droplets. They showed that the wounded beast had gone inside.

Near its mouth the cave was comparatively large, some twenty feet across by about twenty feet high. Daylight filtered into the interior for some yards, beyond which all was darkness. I counted nine separate bee-hives, all of great size, suspended from the roof of the cave close to the entrance. The floor was of rock and appeared to be free of the usual dampness associated with such places. No doubt this accounted for the cave being inhabited by the panther – and the bees, too. For these animals and insects, particularly the former, dislike damp places.

I whispered to my three companions to remain outside and to climb up the sloping rock by the sides of the entrance to a point above the cave, and on no account to go downhill, as that was the direction in which the panther would charge if he passed me. They disappeared, and Kush and I entered the cave.

From that moment Kush seemed to know there was danger ahead. Gone was her erstwhile courage, and she slunk at my heels, gradually falling behind me.

I walked forward as far as I could see in the dim light that filtered in from outside. At most, this might have been for about thirty feet. Then we came to a halt. I could go no further as, not anticipating that my quarry would enter such a cave, I had not brought my torch with me from the village.

There were now two alternatives, either to try to arouse the wounded animal, or to return to Sivanipalli for the torch, telling the men to keep watch from their position of comparative safety above to guard against the panther slinking out before I came back. I should, of course, have followed the second course. Not only was it safer, but more sure. I suppose, really, I felt too lazy to go all that way back and return again. So I thought I would give the first plan a trial and if possible save myself the trouble of a long walk.

THE BLACK PANTHER OF SIVANIPALLI

I whistled and shouted loudly. Nothing happened. I shouted again. Kush, who had been whimpering, then started to bark. Still nothing happened.

The cave had narrowed down to about half its dimensions at the entrance. Only silence rewarded our efforts. The deep, dark interior was as silent as the grave.

Had the wounded animal died inside? This seemed unlikely, as there was no evidence that the panther had lain down again after the first rest he had taken before crossing the Anekal Vanka stream. Had he left the cave before our arrival? This might easily have happened; but again there was no evidence to suggest that such was the case.

I looked around for something to throw. Just one large stone lay close to my feet. I picked it up in my left hand and found it heavy.

I am left handed, for throwing purposes, although I shoot from the right shoulder. I had already cocked my rifle, and, balancing it in the crook of my right arm, threw the stone underarm with as much force as I could muster. It disappeared into the blackness of the cave. I heard it strike the rock floor with a dull thud and then clatter on in a series of short bounces.

The next instant there came the all-too-familiar series of coughing roars as the panther catapulted itself at me out of the darkness. Being a black panther, I could not see it till it emerged from the gloom, two or three yards in front of my rifle. I fired – but the impetus of its charge made the panther seem to slide forward towards me. I fired again. The confines of the cave echoed and re-echoed with the two reports.

Then all hell was let loose. The sound of the bees, which had been registering all this while almost subconsciously on my hearing as a faint humming drone, rose suddenly to a crescendo. The daylight coming in at the entrance to the cave became spotted with a myriad black, darting specks, which increased in number as the volume of sound rose in intensity. The black objects hurled themselves at me. The air was alive with them.

I had aroused the wrath of the bees. Gone was all thought of the panther as I whipped off my khaki jacket, threw it around my exposed back and face and doubled for the entrance.

The bees fell upon me as an avalanche. They stung my hands. They got through the folds of the jacket and stung my neck, my head, my face. One even got down under the collar of my shirt and stung my back.

The stings were horribly painful.

I slid down the sloping rock up which we had climbed just a short while before. As from far away, I could hear Kush yelping in anguish. As fast as I moved, my winged tormentors moved faster; the air was thick with them as they dive-bombed me mercilessly. I remembered comparing them to Japan's suicide pilots, who sacrificed their lives and their machines by literally throwing themselves upon the enemy. Similarly, each bee that stung me that day automatically sacrificed its life. For the end of every bee's sting is barbed, and in trying to extricate the point after it has stung an enemy the insect tears out its sting, with the venom sac attached. These remain embedded in the skin of the victim. Thus, in stinging, the bee does irreparable damage to itself, from the effects of which it dies very soon.

I reached the foot of the sloping shelf with the bees still around me. In desperation I crawled under the thickest lantana bush that was available. Always had I cursed this shrub as a dreadful scourge to forest vegetation and a pest to man, encroaching as it always does on both jungles and fields, in addition to being an impediment to silent and comfortable movement along game trails; but at that moment I withdrew my curses and showered blessings on the lantana instead. It saved my life. For bees must attack and sting during flight, another resemblance they bear to the aforementioned dive-bombers. Clever as they are, they have not the sagacity to settle down and then creep forward on their feet to a further attack. The code with them is to dive, sting and die. The closeness of the network of lantana brambles prevented their direct path of flight on to my anatomy. And so I was delivered from what would have been certain death had the area just there been devoid of the pestiferous lantana I had so often cursed before.

For no matter how fast I had run, the bees would have flown faster and descended in their thousands upon me.

All the nine hives had been thoroughly disturbed by now, and the buzzing of angry bees droned and drummed in the air above me. I lay still and silent under the protecting lantana, smarting from the many stings the creatures had inflicted on me during my flight.

It took over two hours for the droning to subside and for the bees to settle down to work once more. I felt very sleepy and would have dozed were it not that the pain of the stings kept me awake. The hot burning sensation increased as my skin swelled around each wound.

It was three in the afternoon before I could crawl out of the lantana and wend my way downhill to the road; from there I walked to Kundukottai village. There I found my three followers. They had almost completely escaped the attention of the bees at their vantage point above the entrance to the cave. The bees had evidently concentrated their attack on the moving enemies immediately before them – myself and poor Kush, who was also with the three men now. She had been badly stung, and I had no doubt that the panther had also received their close attention.

All of us walked to the car where I had left it the day before. After we had piled in, I set out for Denkanikotta, where there was a Local Fund Hospital and Dispensary. It was quite late in the evening when we roused the doctor. He took us to his surgery in the hospital and with the aid of a pair of tweezers removed the stings embedded in Kush and myself. We had received, respectively, nineteen and forty-one barbs from those little demons in the cave. The doctor applied ammonia to our wounds.

We spent that night in the forest bungalow at Denkanikotta. The beds there are of iron with no mattresses. So I lay in an armchair. The three men slept on the verandah with Kush.

The stings brought on an attack of ague and fever. Kush suffered, too, and I could hear her whimpers. My neck, face and hands were still swollen. One bee had succeeded in registering a sting not far from the corner of my left eye, causing it partially to close.

Dawn made me look a sorry sight with my swollen eye and puffy face as I stood before the one blurred mirror the bungalow boasted.

We waited till past ten and then drove back to the ninth milestone. Retracing our steps – but this time along cattle and game trails where walking was comparatively easy – we came to the place below the rock shelf where we had stood the day before.

The bees were once again busy at their hives. All was peaceful and serene.

Leaving the three villagers, I climbed the slope with Kush for the second time and cautiously approached the cave. I knew I was safe from the bees unless I disturbed them again. And I was almost sure my two shots the previous day had killed the panther. Even if they had not, the bees would have completed that work.

I was right. Lying a few paces inside, and curled into a ball, was the black panther, dead and quite stiff. Kush stayed a yard away from it, sniffing and growling. I put my hand over her mouth to quieten her for fear of disturbing those dreadful bees and bringing them down upon us once more.

Walking out of the cave, I beckoned to the men to come up to me. Together we hauled the panther down the slope. The herdsman, who carried a knife, then lopped off a branch to which we tied its feet with lengths of creeper vine. All four of us then shouldered the load and carried it to the waiting car, where I slung the dead animal between bonnet and mudguard.

At the Denkanikotta forest bungalow I removed the skin. It was a male panther, of normal size, measuring six feet seven inches in length. The rosettes showed up distinctly under the black hairs that covered them. It was the first – and incidentally the only – black panther I have ever shot.

It was difficult to detect the beestings, embedded in the black hair, but I told the men to make a careful count of the barbs they extracted, which I personally checked. There were 273 stings in that animal, confirmed by the number of barbs extracted. There must have been many more that escaped our attention.

I rewarded the men for their services and returned to Bangalore well compensated for the punishment I had received from the bees – for I had a black panther skin, which is something very uncommon – and I had a wonderfully sagacious dog, Kush, whom I purchased from her owner for seven rupees.

There is one thing I nearly forgot to mention. You will remember that I had discovered two separate blood marks at the spot where the panther had stopped to drink in the Anekal Vanka stream. One of them had shown signs of greater bleeding than the other, and because I had fired only one shot I had wondered about it at the time. The reason was now quite clear. My one bullet, aimed between the eyes, had missed its mark, had furrowed past the temple and ear and embedded itself in the animal's groin. The second wound was the one that had bled severely. The first was only superficial. Evidently the body had been slightly twisted and crouched for the spring as I had fired that night. Just in time.

Of the two shots fired in the cave, one (the first) had struck the panther in the chest, and the other, as the panther skidded towards me, had entered the open mouth and passed out at the back of the neck.

CHAPTER 11

The Man-Eating Panther
of the Yellagiri Hills

KENNETH ANDERSON

"Every panther differs from any other panther. Some panthers are very bold; others are very timid. Some are cunning to the degree of being uncanny; others appear quite foolish. I have met panthers that seemed almost to possess a sixth sense, and acted and behaved as if they could read and anticipate one's every thought. Lastly, but quite rarely, comes the panther that attracts people, and more rarely still, the one that eats them.

"A man-eating beast is generally the outcome of some extraordinary circumstance. Maybe someone has wounded it, and it is unable henceforth to hunt its natural prey – other animals – easily. Therefore, through necessity it begins to eat humans, because they offer an easy prey. Or perhaps a panther has eaten a dead human body which was originally buried in a too-shallow grave and later dug up by jackals or a bear. Once having tasted human flesh, the panther often takes a liking to it. Lastly, but very rarely indeed, it may have been the cub of a man-eating mother, who taught it the habit."

Kenneth Anderson *"The Panther's Way"*, 1959

It was mid-afternoon. The tropical sun blazed overhead, a veritable ball of fire. The jungle lay still and silent under its scorching spell. Even the birds and monkeys that had chattered all morning were now quiet, lulled to sleep in the torpid air.

Beneath the dark shadows of the forest trees some relief was to be found from the golden glare, even though the shadows themselves throbbed and pulsated in that temperature. Not the least movement of the air stirred the fallen leaves that thickly carpeted the jungle floor, forming Nature's own luscious blanket of crisp yellow-brown tints. When the monsoons set in, these same crisp leaves would be converted into mouldering manure, which in course of time would serve to feed other forest trees, long after the jungle giants from which they had fallen had themselves crashed to earth.

The heavy stillness was occasionally broken by a hollow sound from the wooden bells hanging from the necks of a herd of cattle that had been driven into the jungle for grazing. These wooden bells serve two purposes. The first and main object is to enable the herdsmen to locate in the thick underbrush the whereabouts of the animals that wear them. The second object is to frighten off any carnivora that becomes disposed to attack the wearers. Quite often the second purpose is successfully achieved, as tigers and panthers are suspicious animals and hesitate to attack a prey from whose neck is suspended a strange wooden object emitting queer sounds. But sometimes, again, the ruse does not succeed, depending upon the nature of the particular tiger or panther concerned, and even more on its hunger at the given moment.

This particular afternoon was to witness one such exception. A fat and brown young bull was browsing on the outskirts of the herd, munching mouthfuls of grass beneath the shade of a clump of ficus trees. With each mouthful that it tore from the ground it would raise its head a little to gaze in idle speculation at the surrounding jungle, while its jaws worked steadily, munching the grass. Nothing seemed to stir and the brown bull was at peace with itself and the world.

It would not have felt so complacent, however, if it had gazed behind. Not a rustle rose as a tuft of grass parted to show two malevolent green eyes that stared with concentrated longing at the fat brown bull. The eyes were those of a large male panther of the big forest variety, and his heavy body, nearly equalling that of a tigress in dimensions, was pressed low to the ground, the colouring of his rosettes merging naturally with the various tints of the grasses.

Slowly and noiselessly the panther drew his hind legs to a crouching position. His muscles quivered and vibrated with tenseness. His whole form swayed gently, to gain balance for the death charge that was to follow.

Then, as a bolt from the blue, that charge took place. As a streak of yellow and black spots, the heavy body of the panther hurtled through the air and, before the brown bull was aware that anything was happening, the cruel yellow fangs buried themselves in its jugular. For a moment the bull struggled to maintain his equilibrium with its forefeet apart, hoping to gallop into the midst of the grazing herd. But with his air supply cut off, and his lifeblood jetting from the torn throat, his resistance was but momentary. He crashed to earth with a thud, all four feet lashing out desperately in an attempt to kick off the attacker. The panther adroitly squirmed his body out of reach of the lashing hooves, but never released his merciless grip on the bull's throat. A snorting gurgle burst from the gaping mouth of the stricken animal, the feet kicked less vigorously, and then his terror-stricken eyes slowly took on a glazed and lifeless expression as death came within a few minutes of the attack.

Thus did Nathan, the herdsman, lose one of his best beasts, as the rest of the herd, alarmed by the noise made by the dying bull, galloped through the jungle for safety to the forest line that eventually led to the village, a couple of miles away.

But this was not to be Nathan's only loss. In the next three months he lost four more of his cattle, while the other two herdsmen who lived in the same village each lost a couple. On the other hand, the panther responsible for these attacks concluded, and no doubt quite justifiably, that he had found a locality where food was plentiful and easy to get. He decided to live nearby in preference to moving through the forest in his normal hunt for game, which was far more arduous anyhow.

The monsoons then came and with the heavy rains pasture grew up everywhere and it became unnecessary to drive the herds of cattle into the jungle for grazing. Grass sprang up near the village itself, and in the few adjacent fields, and the herds were kept close to the village where they could be more carefully watched.

This change, of course, was not relished by the panther, and he became bolder, as he was forced by circumstances to stalk the herds in the new pastures.

The forest thinned out in the vicinity of the village, while the fields themselves were completely treeless. This made the panther's approach more and more difficult, and often enough the herdsmen saw him as he tried to creep towards their charges. On such occasions they would shout, throw stones at him and brandish the staves they carried. These demonstrations would frighten him away.

Then his hunger increased, and he found that he must choose between abandoning the village herds altogether as prey and go back to stalking the wild animals of the forests, or adopting a more belligerent policy towards the herdsmen.

The panther decided to adopt the latter policy.

One evening he crept as far as possible under cover and then dashed openly towards the nearest cow. Two herdsmen, standing quite near, saw him coming. They shouted and waved their sticks, but his charge never faltered till he had buried his fangs in the cow's throat. The herdsmen stood transfixed for the few minutes it took for the cow to die. Then they began to hurl stones and invectives at the spotted aggressor while he lay with heaving flanks across the still-quivering carcass of his prey.

When the stones thudded around, the panther let go his grip on the cow and with blood-smeared grout growled hideously at the men, his evil countenance contorted and his eyes blazing with hatred. Faced with that hideous visage and those blood-curdling growls the herdsmen ran away.

At this stage of affairs the villagers requested the local forester to do something to help them; otherwise to enlist help from some other quarter. The forester, whose name was Ramu, had done a bit of shooting himself and owned a single-barrelled .12 bore breech-loading gun. Although it was part of his duties as the representative of the government to check poachers, he himself was accustomed to indulge in a little poaching over waterholes and saltlicks, his quarry being the various kinds of deer that visited such spots, or an occasional jungle pig. As often as was possible he avoided letting his subordinates, the forest guards, know of these surreptitious activities, but when that was not possible he made sure of the guards' silence by giving them a succulent leg from the animal he had shot, together with a string of dire threats of what he would do to them if a word about it was breathed to the Range Officer. Despite all these precautions, however, the Range Officer had come to know of Ramu's favourite pastime. He was a conscientious young officer, keen to uphold the government's policy of game preservation, and tried to catch his subordinate in the act. But that worthy had so far succeeded in keeping a clean official slate. Perhaps he was too wily, or his threats to the guards so fearsome that the R.O. had not yet succeeded.

So far Ramu had not tried his weapons against any of the larger carnivora, and when the villagers approached him for help to shoot the panther he was not over keen to tackle the proposition. But the villagers persisted in their requests, and soon it was made very evident to Ramu that his honour was at stake, for he could not delay indefinitely with vague excuses of being too busy to come to the village, or of having run out of stock of ammunition and so forth.

Therefore Ramu arrived at the village one morning carrying his weapon. He was hailed as the would-be saviour of the situation and immediately took full advantage of the fact by settling down to a very hearty meal provided by the villagers. After washing this down with a lot of coffee, he belched contentedly and announced his intention of indulging in a nap for an hour before tackling the business for which he had come.

Ramu awoke a couple of hours later, by which time it was past mid-day. He then demanded of the headman that a goat should be provided as bait. This was done and Ramu set out for the jungle, accompanied by five or six villagers.

Being the forester in charge of the section he was well acquainted with the locality and had already selected, in his mind, the tree on which to build his machan. This was a very large banyan, growing conveniently at the point where the track from the village and the forest fire line met. It also happened that a nullah[1] intersected the fire line near the same spot. The panther was known to traverse all three of these approaches, as had been evidenced by his frequent pug-marks, so that Ramu's choice was indeed a wise one; for if the panther walked along the fire line or came up the nullah he could not help spotting his goat, while he himself, in the machan, could see up and down both these approaches as well as part of the track leading to the village.

On this tree, then, Ramu instructed the villagers who had accompanied him to build a machan twenty feet or so off the ground, and being well skilled in the art of making hideouts himself, contrived to conceal it cleverly with leaves, so that it would be quite unnoticeable to the panther.

It was past four o'clock that evening before the work was completed. Ramu climbed into the machan and the goat was then tethered by a rope round its neck to a stake that had been driven into the ground.

When the villagers left, the goat, finding itself alone, gazed in the direction of the village path and bleated lustily. Conditions were as perfect as could be, and the panther heard the goat and pounced on it

1 From the Hindi *nl*. A watercourse, not necessarily a dry watercourse, though it is perhaps more frequently indicated in the Anglo-Indian use.

at about six, while the light was still good. Ramu had loaded his gun with an L.G. cartridge which he fired at the panther while the latter was holding the goat to the ground by its throat. There was a loud cough, and the panther somersaulted before dashing off into the undergrowth. The goat, which was already dying from suffocation and the wound inflicted in its throat, was killed outright by a pellet that passed through its ear into the brain.

Ramu waited awhile, then descended the banyan tree and hastily retreated to the village, where he told the people that he was sure he had hit the panther and had no doubt that they would find him dead the next morning.

With daylight a large party of men assembled and, headed by Ramu, went down to the banyan tree. There they found that the goat had been completely eaten during the night by a hyaena. Ramu pointed out the direction in which the panther had leaped and the whole party of men searched in close formation. It was not long before they came upon a blood trail on the leaves of the bushes and lantana, indicating that in truth he had scored a hit. But of the panther there was no sign, although the party followed the trail for over a mile before it eventually petered out.

For two months after this no fresh attacks on cattle or goats were recorded, and everyone, including Ramu, was sure that the panther had gone away into some thicket and died.

Then one evening a lad of about sixteen years was returning to the village along the same forest line. He was alone. Coming around a bend he saw a panther squatting on his haunches about twenty yards away, looking directly at him. He halted in his tracks, expecting the panther to make off as an ordinary panther would do. But this panther did nothing of the kind. Instead, he changed his position to a crouch and began to snarl viciously.

The boy turned around and ran the way he had come, and the panther pursued him. Luckily, at the place he overtook the boy, a piece of rotting wood happened to be lying across the forest line. As the panther jumped on his back and bit through his shoulder near the neck, the boy was borne to earth by the weight, and in falling saw the piece of rotting wood. Terror and desperation lent strength to his hands and an unusual quickness to his mind. Grasping the wood, he rolled sideways and jammed the end into the panther's mouth. This caused the panther to release his hold, but not before he had severely scratched the boy's arm and thighs with his claws. Springing to his feet, the boy lashed out at him again; this unexpected retaliation by his victim caused the panther to lose courage and he leaped into the bushes. Still grasping the wood that had saved his life, and with blood streaming down his chest, back, arms and legs, the boy made a staggering run for the village.

This was the first attack made upon a human being. The next followed some three weeks later, and this time the panther did not run away. It happened that a goatherd was returning with his animals when a panther attacked them and seized upon one. The herdsman was poor and the herd represented all his worldly wealth. So he tried to save his goat by screaming at the panther as he ran towards him, whirling his staff. It was a brave but silly thing to have done, knowing that a panther was in the vicinity that had recently attacked a human being without provocation. He paid for his foolish bravery with his life, for the panther left the goat and leapt upon him to clamp his jaws firmly in his throat.

The goats ran back to the village. Seeing no herdsman returning with them, some of the villagers wondered what had occurred, but for the moment did not attach any significance to what they had noticed. It transpired that this herdsman was alone and had no relatives so that it was nearly an hour later and growing dusk before his absence was really accepted as a fact, and it became evident that something had happened to him. It was too late by then to do anything.

Next morning the villagers gathered in a party of about thirty persons, armed with clubs and staves, and left the village to try to find the goatherd. They went down the track leading from the village to the jungle. The hoof marks of the herd of goats as they had run back to the village the previous evening were clearly visible along the trail. They proceeded a little further and there they came upon the spot where the panther had made the attack. Clearly impressed in the dusty earth were the pug marks of the large spotted cat. There was also a distinct drag mark where the panther had hauled his victim away. Scattered at intervals were a few drops of blood from the throat of the man that had trickled to the ground. But the earth away from the track was sun-baked and hard and had absorbed the blood, and it was difficult to locate, though the drag mark was quite clear.

The panther had taken his victim off the track along which the man had been driving his goats, and had hauled the body into the jungle. But he had not gone very far from where he had originally made his kill, and within about a hundred yards the group of villagers discovered the body of the victim. The chest and a small portion of one thigh had been eaten. Thus the man-eater of the Yellagiris came into existence.

The Yellagiris are a crescent-shaped formation of hills lying immediately to the east of Jalarpet Junction railway station on the Southern Railway. The opening of the crescent faces away from the Junction, while its apex, so to speak, rises abruptly some three thousand feet above sea level about two miles from the station. A very rough zig-zag path winds up the steep incline, and in places one has to clamber from boulder to boulder.

Many years ago – in 1941 in fact – I had purchased a farm of small acreage at the top of this ridge. I had intended keeping this farm, which is about ninety-five miles from Bangalore, as a weekend resort, but had not found the time to visit it regularly. As a result, the open land was quickly being encroached upon by the ever-prolific lantana shrub.

I had decided to visit this place for about three days to supervise the removal of the lantana, and when I made this visit I happened to arrive a few days after the death of the goatherd. The coolies I had engaged for the work told me about the panther, of which no news had been published in any of the newspapers. They assured me that it continued to haunt the precincts of the village, for they had again seen its pug marks only the previous day.

The news interested me and I thought I might as well make an attempt to bag the animal. I had brought neither of my rifles with me, but only my twelve-bore shotgun, as the Yellagiris abound in junglefowl and during the few visits I had made there I had always shot a couple each time for the pot. Further, with this object in view, I had brought along with me only two L.G. cartridges for emergencies, the rest being number six shot for the junglefowl. Therefore I would have to make sure of the panther with the only two L.G. shells available.

I stopped work on the lantana about midday and went back with the labourers to reconnoitre the ground. It was much as I had expected. The jungle fell away into a narrow belt of lantana which ceased only at the few fields that bordered the village. Clearly visible on a footpath at the end of one of these fields was the trail of a panther – a fairly large adult male, judging from his pugs. He had passed that way only the night before.

I went to the village and introduced myself to the Patel, or headman, whom I had never met before, and told him how I came to be there. He expressed great pleasure at my presence and was most enthusiastic in his promises of every cooperation. We held a discussion and I told the Patel that I would like to buy a goat to tie up as a bait in the initial stage of my operations against the panther.

And here was where the Patel's cooperation was needed, as no goats were available in his village. It was only with much difficulty and considerable delay that he was able to procure one for me from a neighbouring hamlet, a kid that was small enough in size to ensure that it would bleat when tied up. The Patel himself accompanied me, and four other men, one of them leading the goat, the rest carrying hatchets with which to construct a machan.

They led me back along the track to the place where the herdsman had been attacked, and finally to the spot at which they had found his remains. It was densely overgrown with small bushes of the *Inga dulcis* plant, known as the 'Madras thorn' or 'Korkapulli' tree. It was out of the question to sit on the ground there, as the thorns grew so close together as to prevent one from seeing any animal beyond a distance of a couple of yards. So we were compelled to retrace our steps along the track for about a quarter of a mile.

There we came upon quite a large and leafy jak-fruit tree, which, with its thick leaves growing in profusion, seemed to provide the ideal setting for the construction of a machan. At about the height of eight feet the first branch led off the main stem of the tree. The third branch after that extended over the track itself and bifurcated conveniently at about fifteen feet from the ground.

Across this bifurcation I instructed my followers to build the machan. This they set about doing by first lopping small branches off the neighbouring tree and removing the leaves. Then they laid the lopped sticks across the bifurcation, tying them to the two arms with vines cut from the jungle. By this means they had soon made a platform about four feet long by three feet wide. This would be sufficient for me to sit on. Finally, the four sides of the machan were well camouflaged with the leaves they had just removed from the small branches they had cut down to build the base of the machan. We also took great care to conceal the base of the platform itself with leaves, so that to a panther standing anywhere around at any angle, or even directly below, nothing would be visible of the occupant sitting in the machan, nor would anything seem to be out of place to arouse his suspicions unduly.

I got one of the men to make a stake out of a piece of wood, sharpened it a little at one end and then hammered it into the hard ground with a boulder at a distance of just over twenty feet from the machan, keeping in mind the fact that I was using a shotgun.

When all this was ready I climbed into the machan myself and made an opening in the leaves to face the stake, and in such a position that I would have a clear view of the goat and a small portion of the ground around it. By the time we were ready it was nearly five in the evening.

As I have already stated, I had not come to the Yellagiris to shoot big game, so I had not brought my night equipment, the torch that I used to clamp to the barrel of my rifle. Instead, I had brought a small two-cell affair which I only used in camp. It threw only a diffused beam and was quite inadequate for the work which I now had in hand. Further, having no clamp, I would have to hold the torch itself in my left hand and close to the barrel of the gun. The outlook was not so good, since I had come during the moonless period of the month and would have to rely on sounds and my own senses to judge the presence and exact where-abouts of the panther in the darkness, should he turn up.

Bearing all these facts in mind, I settled down in the machan and made myself as comfortable as possible. Then I instructed the men to tether the goat to the stake and walk back to the village, talking loudly to each other. Not only would their withdrawal in this fashion cause the goat to begin bleating as it saw them going away, but should the panther be watching anywhere in the vicinity, their noisy departure, coupled with the bleating of the goat, would induce him to come out early to dinner.

According to instruction, the men tied the goat to the stake and began to walk back in the direction of the village, talking loudly. The goat immediately strained at the rope that held it to the stake and started to bleat so loudly and persistently that I mentally congratulated the Patel on the choice of the bait he had selected. I became certain that if the panther was anywhere around within a mile of this goat he would surely hear its cries and hasten to his intended victim.

But nothing that I expected came to pass. The goat called persistently and loudly, so much so that by the time the sun had set it had become quite hoarse and its cries dwindled to husky squeaks. Twilight found the goat so hoarse that it appeared to resign itself to the inevitable and a night

Slowly and noiselessly the panther drew his hind legs to a crouching position. His muscles quivered and vibrated with tenseness. His whole form swayed gently, to gain balance for the death charge that was to follow.

182

in the open. Folding its forelegs first, it settled down on the ground and fell asleep. I now knew there was but little chance of the panther locating the goat unless it actually happened to pass by and practically stumble upon it. Still, I decided to wait till about nine o'clock and chance my luck.

The next two and a half hours were like many others that I had spent in the jungle under similar circumstances. The calls of the feathered denizens of the forest had long since died away, at least those that belonged to the day. The only sound that could be heard occasionally was the peculiar low whistle of the 'herdboy' bird. This is a grey night bird, some eight inches in length, which emits a low but very penetrating cry exactly resembling the sounds invariably made by herdsmen as they tend their cattle while grazing in the forest, to keep them together. Hence its name, or to give it its Tamil original, 'maatpaya kurrvi', by which it is known throughout southern India. Incidentally, it is a bird that appears to live only in jungly regions or their immediate vicinity, as I have never come across it in the cultivated areas.

There is nothing more that I can tell you, beyond the fact that at 9.15 p.m. I decided to abandon the vigil. I shone the torch in the direction of the goat, but the spreading beam hardly reached the sleeping animal, which I could just detect as a faint blur as I heard it scramble to its feet. Had the panther attacked that goat I would not have been able to see it properly, so I consoled myself with the thought that perhaps it was just as well the panther had not turned up.

Climbing down from the tree I untied the goat and, taking it in tow, went back to the village, where I left it with one of the men who had helped to build the machan, instructing him to look after it until the next day.

Early the following morning I returned to the village to glean as much additional information about the panther as I could. But there was nothing more that anybody could tell me, beyond the facts already related at the beginning of the story, which I slowly pieced together. Nobody knew exactly from where the panther had come and nobody could suggest any particular locality in which he might be living.

The work on my land occupied the next three days, and each evening of those three days I spent in the same machan, sitting up with different goats as baits till a few hours before midnight. But all those three evenings drew a blank, in that I heard no sound of the panther. Each morning I would scour the vicinity of the machan, the forest lines, and various streambeds, but there were no fresh pug marks of the animal for which I was looking, showing that he had not passed anywhere nearby during those nights. Very probably he had moved off to some distant part of the Yellagiri Hills.

On the fourth morning I left for Bangalore, after handing the village Patel my name and address and money for a telegram which he was to send by a runner to Jalarpet railway station.

Over a month passed. No telegram came and I decided that the panther was not a regular man-eater or had perhaps left the Yellagiri Hills to cross the intervening belt of cultivated plain to reach the much more extensive range of forest that clothed the Javadi Hills. This latter range is a wide one and leads far beyond the Yellagiris in a south-easterly direction towards Tiruvanamalai, which is a sacred hill inhabited by a sage said to be possessed of many gifts.

I was quite wrong, as events were to prove.

Seven weeks passed before the telegram, which I had almost forgotten, arrived. It told me that the mail carrier, who brought the 'tappal' or post, from Jalarpet up the hill to the various villages and settlers at the top, had been killed by the panther.

The telegram did not reach me till after three in the afternoon. Nevertheless, by hurrying I was able to catch the Trichinopoly Express which left Bangalore at seven o'clock and reached Jalarpet at 10.30 p.m. I had brought my petromax lantern with me, and by its bright light walked from the station up the hill to reach the village, eight miles away, just before 2 a.m. Normally I would not have dared to risk that rough and steep boulder-covered track by night with a man-eating panther in the vicinity, but I knew that it would be quite safe as long as I had my petromax burning. My .405 rifle and haversack of equipment strapped to my back, plus the light hanging from my left hand, made quite a sizeable and uncomfortable load up that steep track, and I was drenched in perspiration by the time I reached the top of the hill. The village was still a mile away, and a cold breeze chilled my damp clothes as they dried on my back as I walked along.

I awoke the Patel, who in turn awoke most of the village so that a concourse of a hundred dusky faces and gleaming white teeth surrounded me in the light of the petromax.

The Patel offered me food, which I politely declined, but I told him I would be grateful for some hot tea. This was soon prepared, and while sipping it from a large brass utensil belonging to the Patel, I heard the story he had to tell me.

Actually there was nothing much to tell. After my last visit everybody had been very careful when moving about in the day, particularly in the vicinity of the forest. At night they had remained indoors. Then as the weeks had passed without any further signs of the panther, as always happened, vigilance was correspondingly relaxed.

The mail carrier used to ascend the hill early in the morning, leaving Jalarpet at about 6 a.m. from the small post office situated adjacent to the railway station. All the mail trains passed during the night, from Bangalore as well as from Madras on the east coast and Calicut on the west coast. Postal traffic to the Yellagiris was comparatively small, and the few letters or articles that were destined for the hilltop were placed in individual bags by the sorters on the various mail trains and unloaded at Jalarpet Station. These bags the mail carrier, who was to ascend the hill, would open in order to place all their contents into the one bag he carried up, slung across his shoulders or sometimes balanced on his head.

His one protection – which was intended not as much as a weapon of protection but as an emblem and badge of office, as well as a sound-device to frighten away snakes, was a short spear, on the shaft of which were fitted a number of iron rings. This spear he would carry in his hand, striking the base of it against the ground at every few paces. The rings would jangle against the iron shaft and against each other, making the loud jingling-jangling noise that has been known to the mail carrier for almost a hundred years throughout the length and breadth of India.

On that fateful day the mail carrier had as usual set out from the small post office at Jalarpet at about six o'clock in the morning. But he never reached the top of the hill. The villagers had become accustomed to hearing him and seeing him as he jingled and jangled his daily route through the main street of the village. But that morning they had not heard the familiar sound. With the indifference and apathy peculiar to the East, nobody worried or thought anything about it.

After the midday meal, a party of men had started to descend the hill, bound for Jalarpet. About a quarter of the way down they noticed the rusty colour of dried blood splashed on the rocks that formed the trail. They had stopped to wonder about it, when the sharp eyes of one individual had noticed the mail carrier's spear lying away from the track and near a bush. Guessing what had happened, the whole party turned tail and hurried back to the village. There they had gathered reinforcements, including the Patel, and returned eventually to find the partly eaten corpse of the unfortunate mail carrier.

The Patel had written out the telegram and sent it by the same party of men to be despatched to me from Jalarpet Station. With all the confusion it had not reached me till after three the following evening, a delay of some twenty-four hours, although Jalarpet is just eighty nine miles from Bangalore. I was also informed that the police authorities at Jalarpet had removed the body for inquest and cremation.

By the time all this conversation was over and I had elicited all the information I required, or perhaps it would be more correct to say all the information that the Patel and the villagers knew about the panther, it was past four in the morning. The Patel lent me a rope cot which I carried to the outskirts of the village, where I lay down upon it for a brief sleep of two hours till dawn, when I awoke, not to the familiar calls of the forest, but to the loud yapping of a couple of curs who were regarding me on the rope cot with very evident suspicion and distaste.

As I have said, the Yellagiri Hills do not hold a great deal of regular forest, and there is therefore a complete absence of aboriginal jungle folk of any kind. I realized I would have to rely upon the villagers and myself to try to discover ways and means of locating the panther.

One of the questions I had asked earlier that morning concerned the panther's possible hideout. No definite reply had been given to this, but a couple of cattle grazers had stated that they had on three or four occasions during the past few weeks observed a panther sunning himself in the afternoon on a rocky ledge of a hill named 'Periamalai' or 'Big Hill', to give it its English translation. The Yellagiris themselves form a plateau at the top, and this Periamalai is the one and only hill rising above the level of the plateau and forms the highest peak of the crescent-shaped Yellagiri range. It is nearly 4,500 feet above mean sea level.

I went to the Patel's house and found him still asleep, but he soon woke up and offered me a large 'chumbo', which is a round brass vessel like a miniature water pot, of hot milk to drink. I then asked him to call the cattle tenders who had seen the panther on Periamalai and to ask them to accompany me to the hill and point out the particular ledge which the panther was said to frequent.

It took some time before these two individuals could be persuaded to go with me. They were most unwilling and I could see that they were definitely scared. However, the Patel used his own methods of persuasion, which included threats of retribution if they refused, so eventually I was able to set out accompanied by them.

Periamalai is situated about three miles to the east of the village and in the opposite direction to the path from Jalarpet, which ascends to the west. In all, about five miles lay between this hill and the spot where the unfortunate mailman had been killed. In addition, practically all the land between was cultivated. The jungle covering Periamalai itself receded down the slopes of the Yellagiri range in the direction of that portion of the crescent that faces north. I was not happy about this as I felt that the cattle grazers might have seen another panther entirely, and not the one that had killed the postman.

Arriving at the base of Periamalai, my two companions pointed to a ledge of rock that jutted out some 300 feet above, and stated that that was the spot where they had seen the panther sunning himself on several afternoons. Thick lantana scrub grew from the foot of the hill right up to the base of the ledge and to about halfway up Periamalai, where the regular forest began. I could see that, as was happening with so many of the smaller forest tracks in southern India, the lantana pest was slowly but surely encroaching on the jungle proper and smothering the original trees. Like the Yellagiri range itself, Periamalai is a rocky hill consisting of piles of boulders, and to look for a panther in that sea of lantana and among those rocks would be a hopeless task, as the former was impenetrable.

So I marked out a place under a tree growing at the foot of the hill and told the men that we would return to the village and procure a bait, and that they should come back with it and tie it at the spot I had selected.

Accordingly we went back and the Patel procured for me a donkey. A goat would have been of no use in this case as I did not intend to sit up with it. Should it be killed, the panther would devour it at one meal and there would be nothing left to justify his return the following night, whereas the donkey was big enough to warrant the panther coming back for what remained after the first meal. Against this was the disadvantage that a goat would more readily and quickly attract the panther by its bleating, whereas a donkey would be silent.

But I relied on the fact that if the panther lived anywhere on the hill, from his elevated position he would be able to see the donkey tied on the lower ground. So I borrowed some stout rope and instructed the cattlemen to take the donkey back and tether it at the spot I had already pointed out to them.

This done, the Patel himself and three or four villagers came along with me to point out the place where the mail carrier had been done to death. It turned out to be at a spot about a mile and a half from the village, just where the track from Jalarpet passed through a belt of lantana and rocky boulders. I had, of course, passed the place myself the previous night when ascending the hill with the lantern, but had not noticed the blood in the lantern light. No doubt this had been just as well or my tranquillity would have been greatly perturbed.

We came upon a few dried splashes of blood on the trail, and my companions pointed out to me a spot nearby where the unfortunate man had been dragged and partly eaten. As I have already said, his remains had been removed to Jalarpet for cremation, so that there was nothing to be gained by remaining there any longer.

A cashew-nut tree stood beside the trail about three hundred yards higher up, and beneath this tree I asked the Patel to tie another donkey.

Then we walked back to the village, and I suggested a third donkey be tied at some place where the scrub jungle came closest to the village. The Patel once more used his influence to procure two more donkeys and sent them out by different parties of men to be tied as I had instructed.

It was past one in the afternoon by the time all this had been done, and I realized that there was nothing more for me to do but await events. I could only hope the panther would kill one of the three donkeys that night, provided of course he chanced to come upon it. Since the panther had made but few human kills thus far, it was clear that he was mainly existing upon other meat.

The Patel set a hot meal before me, consisting of rice and dhal curry, mixed with brinjals and onions grown on his land and made tremendously hot with red chillies which had been liberally added. I must say I enjoyed that meal, though the sweat poured down my face in rivulets as a result of the chillies. My host was highly amused at this sight and began to apologize, but I stopped him with the assurance that I did enjoy such a meal. Copious draughts of coffee followed, and when

I finally arose I was a very contented person.

To pass the time I went down to my small farm and pottered about for the rest of that evening. You may be interested to know that this farm of mine consists of only one and a half acres of land, but it is a very compact farm at that. There is a 'marking-nut' tree from which nut a black fluid is extracted for making a marking ink generally used by launderers and dhobis for writing the initials of the owners on the corner of each article they send to the wash. Once marked, this 'ink' cannot be washed out. Three 'jak' trees, which are of a grafted variety, produce fruit weighing from two to twelve pounds each or even more. There are a few guava trees, some peaches and a vegetable garden. The two existing buildings, or 'kottais' as they are called, are mud-walled affairs with thick thatched roofs made from a mixture of jungle grass and the stalks of 'cholam' grain. A small rose and croton garden fronts them. At that time I had about three dozen fowls, including leghorns, rhodes and black minorcas, and a few ducks. My drinking water comes from a small well into which I introduced some fish, which I had originally brought from Bangalore to keep the water clean. A small stream in front forms one of my boundaries, and bamboo trees line the other three sides. Although such a small place, it is extremely 'cosy', and an ideal retreat for a quiet Sunday visit from Bangalore.

About half the land is low lying and borders the stream I have just mentioned. I have tapped some water from this rivulet and grown a variety of black rice, known as 'Pegu' rice and originally imported from Burma. To my knowledge, my farm was one of the very few spots in southern India where this black Burma rice then grew. I knew it had been sown in many places, but its cultivation had proved a failure for one reason or another.

An interesting feature about this farm was a story that one of the two kottais was haunted by the ghost of the brother of the Anglo-Indian lady from whom I had purchased it in 1941, lock, stock and barrel, poultry included, for the sum of Rs 500/–; about £35 in English money. This man had died of a reputedly mysterious disease which I was told occurred in sudden attacks of excruciating pain in his left arm and chest – probably *angina pectoris*. He had been very much attached to the small farm and was said to have spent over twenty five years there after purchasing it as waste land. Then he gave it to his sister, as he had no family of his own. However, as the story went, after his death passing villagers had frequently seen him standing before his kottai in the evenings just as dusk was falling. Thereafter, needless to say, the villagers avoided the place.

His sister told me nothing about the alleged haunting till the day after I had purchased the farm and paid the cash before the Sub-Registrar when I had registered the sale deed, probably thinking the 'ghost' would put me off the transaction. Then she told me that her dead brother would sometimes roam about the two kottais at night, and also that she had clearly seen him many times in the moonlight attending the rose trees which had been his special hobby. She hastened to add that the 'spirit' was quite harmless, made no sound or troublesome manifestation, and just faded away if approached.

I have failed to mention that some very ancient furniture came to me with the kottais: a bed in each building, a broken-down dressing table, two almirahs and some three or four rather rickety chairs. The beds were of the old-fashioned sort, having battens.

I well remember the first night I slept in one of the kottais (incidentally the one in which the brother had died), for it was a rainy night and the roof of the other kottai was leaking. I had spread my bedroll, without mattress, on the battened cot and had lain down to sleep. The hard battens, however, were irksome and pressed against my shoulder blades and back. After failing to woo slumber for some time, I had decided that the floor would be far more comfortable. Of course, there were no electric lights, so I had lighted a candle to enable me to remove the bedroll and place it on the floor, when I had extinguished the candle and lain down to sleep. This time I was successful and had fallen asleep immediately.

I do not know when I awoke. It was pitch dark. Something heavy and cold and clammy moved and rested against my throat, and what seemed like two icy wet fingers extended across either side of my neck.

Now I am not an imaginative person. I am not afraid of the dark. Nor am I superstitious. But in a rush of memory I recollected the dead brother and his ghost, the fact that I had left my torch on the window sill some feet away, and also that I did not know where I had left the matchbox. These thoughts came simultaneously, while the cold clammy wet thing distinctly moved and seemed to press its two extended fingers even more tightly on either side of my throat. I could feel my hair rising. To lie there any longer was impossible. With what seemed superhuman energy I scrambled to my feet and dashed towards the unfamiliar window sill where I had left my torch, crashing over one of the old chairs and breaking it to pieces. Probing wildly in the dark, I at last found that elusive torch. I pressed the button, expecting to see the ghost and its clammy hands, cold from the grave, before me! Instead, there on the floor was quite the largest toad I had ever seen in my life. A huge, black, slimy fellow, almost a foot long. He had come into the kottai because of the rain.

This just goes to show what human nerves can do. Hardly a few seconds earlier I had been scared stiff by the thought of the supernatural and the unknown. Now I laughed to myself as I guided the toad with the toe of my slippered foot to the door of the kottai, and then out into the rain.

Next morning all three donkey baits were alive, and so I spent the day on my land. No one had any news to give about the panther. Another night passed and the following morning found all three of the donkeys still in the land of the living. This time there was a little news. After the death of the mail carrier the post was conveyed up the hill by three men instead of one, the party consisting of the relief mail carrier who had replaced the poor fellow that had been killed, together with two 'chowkidars' – literally, 'watchmen' – who had been pressed into service to accompany him as bodyguards. These were armed with crude spears in addition to the 'emblem of office' spear which had once been the equipment of the deceased mail carrier and now automatically fell to his successor.

These three men excitedly reported at the village that they had seen a panther sunning himself on a ledge of a rock about a quarter of a mile downhill from the place where the previous mail carrier had been done to death.

Upon hearing this news the Patel had despatched a villager to run and tell me. Taking my rifle, I accompanied him back to the village, where both the chowkidars offered to come along with me to point out the rock. We covered the distance of a little over two miles in good time. But only the bare rock ledge stared us in the face. The panther that had been lying there, man-eater or otherwise, had gone, and it was too hot, too rocky and too hopeless to search for him among the piles of boulders. However, the news was encouraging, as it indicated the panther was still in the vicinity. Before returning to the village and my small farm, I once again examined the bait under the cashew tree and mentally selected the branch on which I would fix my machan if occasion arose.

That night brought good luck, though bad for the donkey beneath the cashew nut tree, for the panther killed and ate about half of him during the hours of darkness.

Early next morning this fact was discovered by the party of men whom I had delegated to inspect, feed and water each one of the three baits in turn. They came back and told me, after having taken the precaution to cover the remains of the donkey with branches to protect it from being devoured to the bones by vultures.

I finished an early lunch and with my greatcoat, torch and flask of tea and some biscuits, proceeded to the village, where I readily obtained the loan of a charpoy from the Patel. Four willing helpers carried this to the cashew nut tree, where it was slung up and secured with the ropes we had brought along with us. I personally supervised the camouflaging of the charpoy with small branches and leaves, till it was invisible from every direction, as well as from below. That this job should be done very thoroughly was, I knew, most essential when dealing with man-eating carnivora. The slightest carelessness might make all the difference between success and failure. A leaf turned the other way, with its undersurface showing uppermost, or any portion of the charpoy being visible from any angle, a remnant of twigs or fallen leaves at the base of the tree, any of these would be sufficient to arouse the suspicion of a man-eater, which is always extremely cautious in returning to its kill.

All that I could find was that the machan was rather low, not more than ten feet from the ground. Also that the cashew nut tree was easy to climb. It was about two-thirty in the afternoon when the party of men who had accompanied me left, after I had instructed them to return at dawn in case I did not go back to the village myself during the night.

I sat back on the machan and made myself as comfortable as possible.

It was a sweltering afternoon, the heat being reflected by the boulders that were piled around in all directions. The tree itself afforded little protection from the afternoon sun that beat down upon me. Indeed, I was glad when evening approached and the sun began sinking towards the Mysore plateau to the west. Far below me I could see Jalarpet railway station on the plains, and the puffs of cream-coloured smoke from the shunting-engines in the yard. At intervals a train would arrive or leave, and the whistles of the locomotives could be clearly heard. All else was silent.

Towards dusk a single peacock wailed in the distance and a couple of nightjars flitted around the tree. Except for them there were no signs of any other animals or birds.

Then the shadows of night descended. Sitting on the slope of the hill facing the west, I could see the plains grow dark as if covered by a black mantle, while yet the last vestiges of daylight lingered on the hilltop above me. The lights of Jalarpet began to twinkle one by one, prominent among them being the blue-tinted neon lamps of the station platforms and shunting yards. Here and there I could make out the red and green lights of the railway signals. From the north a train rolled towards Jalarpet, the bright headlamp of the engine cutting a swath of light before it. Then the train encountered an incline and the engine began to labour under its load. "If she can do it . . . I can do it . . . if she can do it . . . I can do it." Her puffs as she struggled to top the rise formed the words in my imagination, and I listened to the clanking of her worn big-end bearings. All these sounds seemed so close to me – and yet they were so far; they were over five miles away at least, as the crow flies.

Darkness fell around me. It was a moonless night. The heavy clouds scuttled across the sky, some of them merging with the tops of the Yellagiri range. No friendly stars shone down, and the darkness became intense. I would have to rely on my sense of hearing.

Insects were conspicuous by their absence, and even the friendly chirp of the wood-cricket was not to be heard. I sat still on the cot. Now and then a passing mosquito buzzed around my head, to settle on some part of my face or hands. Then came the faint sharp sting of pain as it imbedded its needle-pointed proboscis into my skin. I would move my fingers or hand a little, or noiselessly blow against my own face by slightly protruding my lower lip. This would disturb the mosquito, which would either go on its way or fly around in a further effort to take another bite at me.

I am accustomed to sitting up in the jungle on machans or in hideouts and so lost count of the time, for in any case it served no purpose to keep looking at my wrist watch unnecessarily. I could not anyway make time pass quicker.

Thoughts of all kinds creep into a man's mind on such occasions, some pleasant, some otherwise, and some reminiscent. I remember that that evening, for some unaccountable reason, I began thinking up some way of inventing a new sort of bicycle – something that one could propel fast and for long distances with the minimum of effort. Is it not strange what the human mind may think of when it is forced to be idle?

My reveries concerning this bicycle were disturbed by what seemed like a faint sigh. I knew the panther had arrived and was standing over the dead donkey. The muffled sound I had heard had been made by his expelled breath as he slightly opened his mouth.

I reasoned that to switch on my torch and fire at this juncture might be premature. Better to let him settle down to his meal. I wish I hadn't, for in doing so I lost what might have been a successful shot and caused the death of another human being.

I waited expectantly for the sound of the meat being torn, and bones being crunched, which would have assured me that the panther was tucking in at the donkey, but instead I heard nothing. The moments slipped by and then I became uncomfortably suspicious that something had gone wrong.

I know from experience how noiseless any of the carnivora can be when they want to; particularly a panther which can come and go not only soundlessly, but also without being seen, and that too in broad daylight. Under the present conditions of intense darkness this animal might have been a yard away, or a mile away, for all the difference it made in that gloom.

I glanced down at the luminous dial of my watch, which showed that it was twenty minutes to nine. I waited without moving. Nine o'clock came and passed, and then, from a section of boulders to my right, I heard a deep growl, followed in a few seconds by another.

Somehow the panther had become aware of my presence. He could not have smelt me, as panthers have little or no sense of smell. He could not have heard me, for I had made no sound. Therefore, he had either looked up inadvertently and become aware of the machan, or some intuition had warned him. In either case, he now knew a human being was there. He might then have tried climbing up into the tree to pull me down, but as likely as not his sense of self-preservation had warned him that this particular human being was dangerous to him and not of the same sort as the men he had killed.

Of course, this panther might not be a man-eater, although in the light of his present conduct this seemed the less reasonable explanation.

The growls were initially intended as a warning. As they increased they were also clearly meant to bolster up the animal's own courage. Perhaps he would lash himself into a fury after a sufficient number of growls to attack the tree on which I was sitting and try to climb up. As I have had occasion to remark before, panthers frequently do this with monkeys, whom they terrify with a series of loud growls before rushing at the trunk of the tree. Then the monkeys generally fall off or jump down in sheer terror. As likely as not he expected the noise he was making to have the same demoralizing effect on me.

Very soon the growls increased both in volume and tempo. The panther was now making a terrific noise. As I had just thought, he was either trying to frighten me away completely or off my perch; alternatively, he was building up his own courage to rush the tree. I prepared for the latter eventuality.

Some more minutes of this sort of thing went on and then out he came with the peculiar coughing roar made by every charging panther. As he reached the base of the cashew nut tree I leaned over the edge of the cot, pushing aside the camouflaging twigs to point the rifle downwards while depressing the switch of my torch. I knew I had to be quick because, as I have told you, the machan was only about ten feet off the ground and, the tree being easy to climb, the panther would reach me in no time.

As bad luck would have it, one of the camouflaging branches fell down upon the panther. No doubt this served to delay, if not actually to deter, his progress up the tree. But it also served to screen him completely from the light of the torch. As I looked downwards I just saw the branch shaking violently and guessed that it covered the panther.

At that moment I did a foolish thing. Instead of waiting till the animal could break clear of the offending branch, I quickly aimed at the spot where I felt his body would be and pressed the trigger. The report of the shot was followed by the sound of a falling body as the panther

Arriving at the base of Periamalai, my two companions pointed to a ledge of rock that jutted out some 300 feet above . . . where they had seen the panther sunning himself on several afternoons.

198

went hurtling backwards to the ground. For a second I thought I had succeeded in killing him, but that thought lasted only for a second, for no sooner did he touch the ground than he jumped clear of the branch in which he had become entangled, and I caught a momentary glimpse of his yellow form leaping into the undergrowth before I had a chance to work the underlever that would reload my rifle.

I shone the torch at the spot where he had disappeared, but neither sight nor sound of him or his further progress came to me. Silence reigned supreme. He might be lying dead in the bushes, or he might be wounded there, or he might have disappeared and be a long way off. There was no way of knowing.

I continued to shine the torch around for some time and then decided to sit in darkness in the hope of hearing some sound of movement. But there was absolutely nothing. I waited for another hour and then made up my mind to fire a shot into the bushes in the direction in which he had gone, hoping it would elicit some reaction if he were lying there wounded. So, switching on the torch, I fired the rifle at the approximate spot where he had vanished. The crash of the report reverberated and echoed against the hillside, but there was no sound or response from the panther.

A goods train started from Jalarpet and began to climb the gradient to Mulanur on the ghat section that led to Bangalore. The banking engine at the rear, whose duty it was to help by pushing till the top of the gradient was reached, began to push vigorously and its puffing and clanking eclipsed the sounds made by the engine at the front, whose driver was perhaps taking it easy because of the ready help behind him.

I waited until 11.30 p.m. The loud whistling from the engine of the incoming Madras–Cochin express decided me to come down from the tree and go back to my kottai for a comfortable night's sleep. I felt quite safe in doing this as, had the panther been wounded and in the vicinity, he would have responded to the noise of my last shot. Either he was dead or far away. Even if he had been lying in wait, that last shot would have frightened him off.

I came down from the cashew nut tree and by the light of my torch made my way back to the village, where, before going on to my kottai, I related all that had happened to the Patel and the excited villagers.

Early next morning I came back to the village, where at least twenty willing men assembled and offered to help me. They in turn, under my advice and directions, gathered half-a-dozen village curs. Thus, safe and strong in numbers, we proceeded to the cashew nut tree and the site of the previous night's occurrences.

The remains of the donkey had been untouched. A hole in the ground, directly below the tree, showed where my bullet had buried itself in the earth, nor was a speck of blood to be seen anywhere. We thoroughly searched among the bushes into which the panther had disappeared and into which I had fired my second shot, as well as the surrounding boulders and bushes for quite a wide area, but it was clear that I had missed entirely and that my bullet of the night before had failed to score the lucky hit I had hoped for. The panther had got completely away.

Ill tempered and disgusted with myself, I returned with the men to the village, where I told the Patel that my time was up and that I would have to return to Bangalore. However, I asked him to send me another telegram should there be further developments. Then I went to the kottai, gathered my belongings and packed them in my haversack, and soon was repassing the cashew nut tree on my descent to Jalarpet, where I caught the evening express from Madras that got me home by eight-fifteen the same night.

That was the end of the first round of my encounter with the Yellagiri man-eating panther.

Contrary to expectations, I heard nothing more from the Patel. When two months had elapsed I wrote him a letter and received a reply within a few days stating that there had been no further news of the animal. This made me think that it may have relinquished its man-eating habits or have crossed over to the Javadi range of hills which lay scarcely fifteen miles south of the Yellagiris. On the other hand, had the latter been the case I would still have heard through the Press or by Government notification if any people had been killed on the Javadi Hills. I was therefore inclined to the former theory and felt that the panther had given up his tendency to attack human beings. Of course, my chance shot might have found its mark, and the animal may have crept away to die in some secluded place. But this last theory was hardly tenable.

Nine more weeks passed before the next news arrived in the form of a telegram from the Patel, despatched from Jalarpet railway station, stating that the panther had reappeared and once again killed a human being. The telegram asked me to come at once, and with two hours to spare I caught the next train.

This happened to be a slow train which brought me in to Jalarpet station at about half-past eight that night. There was no purpose in my climbing the hill immediately, for there was nothing I could do just then, so I decided to take a few hours' sleep in the waiting room and make the ascent at dawn. This plan did not prove very successful, however. To begin with, the noise of the passing trains disturbed me each time I fell asleep, being a light sleeper. Secondly, the attacks of mosquitoes and bed bugs, with which the chair seemed to abound, impelled me to walk about the platform, which I did till five in the morning, when I set off for the foot of the Yellagiris about two miles away. It was dawn as I began the climb and I reached the Patel's village by 7.15.

My friend the Patel greeted me with his usual hospitality and brass 'chumbo' of heavily milked hot coffee. Then he told me that the panther had attacked and killed a young woman three mornings previously, when she had gone to draw water from a stream running past the base of Periyamalai Hill. He also informed me that the people of the village to which the girl had belonged had arrived shortly afterwards and recovered the remains of the victim for cremation. Apparently the panther had eaten but little of the unfortunate woman, perhaps because it had been disturbed by the party of men searching for her and had not had time to settle down to his meal.

This time I decided to tie a live bait in the form of a goat and sit up over it, as my stay on the Yellagiris could not exceed four days, as I had only that much leave. So the Patel offered to procure one for me from the same neighbouring village where he had got them the last time, but said that it would cost a tidy sum of money – about twenty rupees – as not only were goats scarce on the Yellagiris but their owners in that village, which was about three miles away, had become aware of the demand and had raised their prices accordingly. I agreed and handed over the money, and in the time that it would take for the goat to be brought went down to my farm to see how things were getting along.

At noon, after consuming the cold lunch I had brought with me from Bangalore, I returned to the Patel's village only to find that the goat had not yet arrived.

It was two in the afternoon before the man who had been sent to fetch the animal returned with a black goat that was rather old, in the sense that it was past the stage where it would bleat for a long time when left alone, and so help to attract the panther. Secondly, as I have said, it was a black goat. Black or white goats occasionally cause suspicion among certain panthers. A brown bait, whether goat, dog or bull, is generally the best to use, in that they resemble in colour the wild animals that form the panther's natural food. However, there was no time now to change the goat and I would have to make the best of the circumstances.

The Patel and four or five men accompanied me, the latter carrying axes, ropes and the same charpoy I had used on the last occasion. We reached the village to which the girl had belonged in a little under an hour. There another couple of men joined my party, who offered to point out the exact spot at which the young woman had been killed.

It was perhaps three-quarters of a mile from the village. A stream, bearing a trickle of water, ran from west to east and skirted the base of Periamalai Hill perhaps a half-mile away. This stream was sandy and bordered by a thick out-crop of mixed lantana and wait-a-bit thorns. At the spot where the girl had been attacked a shallow hole had been dug by the villagers to form a pool for watering their cattle when the weather became dry and the rest of the stream ceased to flow. It was to this place that the girl had come for water when she had been killed the previous day. The lantana grew quite close to the pool, and it was evident that the man-eater had stalked her under cover of this thicket, and from there had made his final pounce.

As matters stood, this panther had again confirmed that he was most unusual in his habits, even for a man-eater. He had repeatedly attacked his human victim in broad daylight. Only tigers do this, as man-eating panthers, being inherent cowards at heart, usually confine their activities to the hours of darkness. I was inclined to think that this animal was perhaps already lying up in the thicket before the girl arrived and could not resist the temptation of a meal so readily offered.

With this idea in mind, I went down on hands and knees and began a close examination of the lantana bushes and the ground in the vicinity, where I shortly found confirmation of my theory, for one of the bushes provided ample shelter for a regular lie-up. Beneath it the carpet of dried lantana leaves rendered impossible the chance of finding any visible track, but a faintly prevailing odour of wild animal inclined me to confirm my guess as correct, and that the panther used this place now and then to lie up, as it offered ideal proximity for attack on any prey that might approach the pool to drink.

This was encouraging for, if the panther had used it before, there was every likelihood that he would use it again. Further, as I have already told you, Periamalai Hill lay about half a mile away. The panther might have his regular den among the rocks and caves higher up the hill and would find this lantana lair a most convenient place in which to await the coming of an unsuspecting victim.

As I studied these conditions an idea suddenly came to me. I would create a scene as close as possible to what the panther might expect it to be. I would tether the goat to a stake beside the pool to make it appear like an animal that had come there to drink. And I would forestall the panther's arrival by hiding myself beneath that very same lantana bush. Should he hear the goat, or catch a glimpse of it from higher up the hill, from where it would be clearly visible, he would make straight for this point of attack and would find me waiting for him.

I explained my idea to the Patel and the men who had accompanied me. They thought it clever, but the Patel decided it was foolish, in that it entailed too great a risk. I convinced him that there was really little danger as, due to the denseness of the surrounding lantana and the thickness of the bush itself, the panther would have difficulty in getting at me from any of the sides or rear, and could only reach me through the entrance to this under-cover shelter, while I would be expecting him to arrive from that direction and would be ready. Further, his attention would be concentrated on the goat and he would scarcely suspect an enemy would await him in his own lair.

The stake which we had brought along was accordingly hammered deep into the sand with the aid of a stone from the stream bed. I crept under the bush and took my time in making myself quite comfortable for the night. I also clamped the torch to the barrel of my rifle, and tested it to see that it was in good order. This torch I had lately purchased. It was a three-cell arrangement of the fixed-focus type. Finally, I took a long drink of tea from my water bottle before ordering the men to tether the goat to the stake by its hind legs.

While all these preliminaries were going on the goat had been kept some distance away, so that it should not come to know that a human being was sheltering in the bushes so close by; for once it knew that, there was very little chance of it bleating from a sense of loneliness. On the other hand, if the goat really felt it had been left alone, there was much more reason why it should cry out.

While the goat was being tied I remained perfectly silent. After finishing their job, the Patel and his men went away and I was left by myself to await what might happen.

It was hot and still beneath the lantana, and long before sunset it was quite dark where I was sitting. The goat had bleated a few times at the beginning and then had stopped. I could only hope that it would begin calling again when darkness fell. But I was sorely disappointed. Occasionally I had heard the sounds made by the goat as it kicked and struggled against the tethering rope, but these had now lapsed into silence and I came to the inevitable conclusion that the damned animal had gone to sleep.

Of necessity, in my position I had to keep wide awake and alert the whole night and could not share the goat's slumbers. I envied that blasted goat.

Mosquitoes worried me, and insects of all kinds ran over my body. Bush mice, which are even smaller than the domestic variety, rustled the leaves and crept along the stems of the lantana. Once something long and soft slithered through the dry leaves and along the sides of the bush. It was a snake. Whether harmless or poisonous I could not know. I sat absolutely motionless in spite of the mosquitoes and insects, and the slithering died away.

The panther did not come. No sounds penetrated the silence under the bush, not even the calls of a night bird. Time moved on its long and tedious course. The luminous hands of my wristwatch very slowly clocked the passing hours. I felt drowsy but dared not give in to my inclination to close my eyes even for a few fitful seconds. I tried to think of other things and other events to get my mind off the panther. The only thing I could think of was to damn the goat.

The greying light of a new day gradually filtered in, not even heralded by the call of a junglefowl, peafowl, or any other bird. I came out of that bush the most disgusted man in the whole of India. The goat, which had been lying curled up and fast asleep by the stake, lazily got to its feet, stretched leisurely, wagged its stumpy tail and regarded me in a quizzical fashion as much as to say, "Come now, who is the real goat, you or me?" Knowing the answer, I refrained from a spoken confession.

Instead, I untethered that wretched animal, which followed me back to the village where the Patel lived. That worthy, with the same party of men who had accompanied us the day before, was just about to set forth to see how I had fared. Telling him to return the black goat, I said that I would snatch a few hours' sleep and then go myself to find a more satisfactory bait. I went to my kottai and slept till noon.

I was feeling hungry when I awoke, so I opened a tin of salmon, which I ate with some bread I had brought with me from Bangalore. The bread had become rather dry, but was improved by the tinned butter I spread thickly upon it. This served to fill me for lunch. I had already set my portable Primus stove to boil water for tea and the beverage was indeed refreshing. While eating my lunch I brewed a second kettle of tea to put into my water bottle. Gathering the necessary equipment for another night's vigil, I returned to the Patel's village. Fortunately the weather was warm as the previous night, so that an overcoat was unnecessary.

I took the Patel along with me to add force to my argument. and walked to the village where the goats were available. There, after some picking and choosing, followed by some red-hot bargaining, I was able to select a half-grown animal that was more likely to bleat. It was past 3.30 p.m. when we set out for the place where I had sat up the night before, but really there was no hurry, as the spot had already been selected and there was no machan to fix.

Before five o'clock I had crept into the bush, the new goat was tethered and the men were on their way back.

Hardly were they out of sight and earshot than the goat began to bleat, and he kept this up incessantly. I silently congratulated myself on my selection.

With evening it again became quite dark beneath the lantana, the goat called loudly and I waited expectantly for the panther. An hour passed. Then I heard an almost imperceptible rustle, the faintest sound of a dry twig being trodden upon, and I sensed the panther was coming. The crucial moment had almost arrived. Now I had to be careful not to shine the torch before the panther was fully in view. If I did so, I knew he would disappear. On the other hand, if I delayed too long, he might see me first and perhaps make a charge, or even vanish.

With all my senses at full stretch, I waited. There were no fresh rustlings or other sounds. Then I heard a faint hiss. Instinctively I knew the panther had seen or sensed me. He had curled back his lips in a snarl, preparatory to the growl that would most likely follow. That curling of his lips had occasioned the slight hissing sound I had heard. It was now or never. My thumb went down on the switch button of the torch. Its beam sprang right into the twin reddish-white eyes of the panther. I could clearly see his face and chest perhaps ten feet away. Aiming quickly at the throat I pressed the trigger of the Winchester. The panther appeared to come forward a pace. Then he reared up on his hind legs, but not before my second bullet took him full in the chest. He fell over backwards out of sight and threshed the bushes for a few seconds. Next came the unmistakable gurgling sounds of a dying animal; then silence.

I waited another half-hour before deciding to take the risk of leaving the bush. I thought it reasonably safe to do so, as I was almost sure the panther was dead. Holding the cocked rifle before me, I crawled out of cover and stood beside the goat. My first impulse was to cut it loose and take it in tow along with me. Then the thought came to my mind that the panther I had fired at might not have been the man-eater after all, but just an ordinary animal. If that were so, I would need to exercise every precaution in returning to the Patel's village in the darkness and could not afford to hamper myself by leading a goat that would necessarily distract my attention. So I left it where it was and set out for the Patel's abode, where I arrived after slow and cautious walking. The people were still awake and I told them what had happened. Then I went to my kottai for a sound night's sleep.

Next morning we found the panther where he had fallen. An old male, with a somewhat scraggy and pale coat, he showed every sign of being the man-eater, for his canine teeth were worn down with old age and his claws were blunt and frayed.

But only time would tell whether I had bagged the real culprit.

By noon I was on my way down the hill with his pelt.

Many years have elapsed since that incident took place, but no more people have been killed on either the Yellagiri or Javadi ranges, and so I am reasonably sure I succeeded that night in bringing the man-eater to bag.

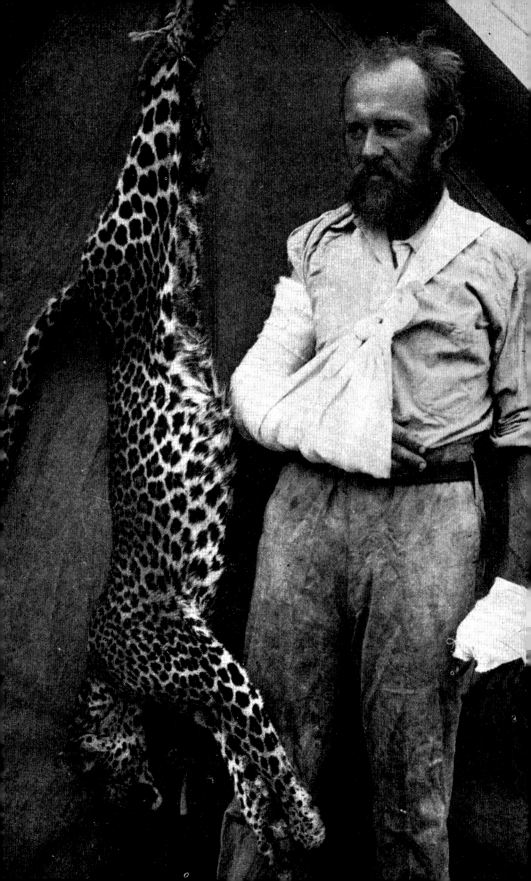

CHAPTER 12

The Wounded Leopard

CARL E. AKELEY

Carl E. Akeley was an extraordinary man. In the 1923 edition of his best-selling In Brightest Africa *he has described an almost unbelievable encounter with a leopard on an 1896 zoological expedition in British Somaliland for The Field Columbia Museum of Chicago. He eventually killed the animal with his bare hands – an event that has never been done before or since. Akeley's sculptures, and his brilliant taxidermy, can still be seen in the African and Roosevelt Halls of the American Museum. Living in Africa, in pursuing his work for the Museum, Akeley came close to death many times. The following fearless encounter with a leopard will go down in history as an example of how bravery can sometimes triumph over the odds.*

"When only half a mile from camp I met an old hyena who was loafing along after a night out. He looked like a good specimen, but after I shot him, one look at his dead carcase was enough to satisfy me that he was not as desirable as I had thought, for his skin was badly diseased. I had very good reason to think of this very hard later in the day. A little farther along I shot a good warthog for our scientific collection. Leaving the specimen where it lay, I marked the spot.

"We returned to camp later in the afternoon and after a little rest and refreshment I started out again with only the pony boy and carrying the necessary tools to get the head of the warthog that I had shot in the morning. We had no difficulty in finding the place where I had shot him, but there was nothing to be seen of the pig. The place was strewn with vulture features, but surely vultures could not make away with the head. A crash in the bushes at one side led me in a hurry in that direction and a little later I saw my pig's head in the mouth of a hyena travelling up the slope of a ridge out of range. That meant that my warthog specimen was lost.

"The sun was setting, and with a little to console us the pony boy and I started for camp. As we came near to the place where I had shot the diseased hyena in the morning, it occurred to me that perhaps there might be another hyena about the carcase, and feeling a bit "sore" at the tribe for stealing my warthog, I thought I might pay off the score by getting a good specimen of a hyena for the collections. The pony boy led me to the spot, but the dead hyena was nowhere in sight. There was the blood where he had fallen, and in the dusk we could make out a trail in the sand where he had been dragged away.

"Advancing a few steps, a slight sound attracted my attention, and glancing to one side I got a glimpse of a shadowy form going behind a bush. Without a sight of what I was shooting at, I shot hastily into the bush. The snarl of a leopard told me what kind of a customer I was taking chances with. A leopard is a cat and has all the qualities that gave rise to the 'nine lives' legend. To kill him you have got to kill him clear to the tip of his tail. Added to that, a leopard, unlike a lion, is vindictive. A wounded leopard will fight to a finish practically every time, no matter how many chances it had to escape. Once aroused, its determination is fixed on fight, and if a leopard even gets hold, it claws and bites until its victim is in shreds. All this was in my mind, and I began looking about for the best way out of it, for I had no desire to try conclusions with a possibly wounded leopard when it was so late in the day that I could not see the sights of my rifle. My intention was to leave it until morning and if it had been wounded, there might be a chance of finding it. I turned to the left to cross to the opposite bank of a deep, narrow 'tug' and when there I found that I was on an island where the 'tug' forked, and by going along a short distance to the point of the island I would be in a position to see behind the bush where the leopard had been stopped. But what I had started the leopard was intent on finishing. While peering about I detected the beast crossing the 'tug' about twenty yards above me. I again began shooting, although I could not see to aim. However, I could see where the bullets struck at the sand spurted up beyond the leopard. The first two shots went above her, but the third scored. The leopard stopped and I thought she was killed. The pony boy broke into a song of triumph which was promptly cut short by another song such as only a thoroughly angry leopard is capable of making as it charges. For just a flash I was paralyzed with fear, then came power for action. I worked the bolt of my rifle and became conscious that the magazine was empty. At the same instant I realised that a solid point cartridge rested in the palm of my left hand, one that I had intended, as I came up to the dead hyena, to replace with a soft nose. If I could but escape the leopard until I could get the cartridge into the chamber!

"As she came up the bank on one side of the point of the island, I dropped down the other side and ran about to the point from which she had charged, by which time the cartridge was in place, and I wheeled – to face the leopard in mid-air. The rifle was knocked flying and in its place was eighty pounds of frantic cat. Her intention was to sink her teeth into my throat and with this grip and her forepaws hang on to me while with her hind claws she dug out my stomach, for this pleasant practice is the way of leopards. However, happily for me, she missed her aim. Instead of getting my throat she was to one side. She struck me high in the chest and caught my upper right arm with her mouth. This not only saved my throat but left her hind legs hanging clear where they could not reach my stomach. With my left hand I caught her throat and tried to wrench my right arm free, but I couldn't do it except little by little. When I got grip enough on her throat to loosen her hold just a little she would catch my arm again an inch or two lower down. In this way I drew the full length of my arm through her mouth inch by inch. I was conscious of no pain, only of the sound of the crushing of tense muscles and the choking, snarling grunts of the beast. As I pushed her further and further down my arm I bent over, and finally when it was almost freed I fell to the ground, the leopard underneath me, my right hand in her mouth, my left hand clutching her throat, my knees on her lungs, my elbows in the armpits spreading her front legs apart so that the frantic clawing did nothing more than tear my shirt. Her body was twisted in an effort to get hold of the ground to turn herself, but the loose sand offered no hold. For a moment there was no change in our positions and then for the first time I began to think and hope I had a chance to win this curious fight. Up to that time it had been simply a good fight in which I expected to lose, but now if I could keep my advantage perhaps the pony boy would come with a knife. I called, but to no effect. I still held her and continued to shove the hand down her throat so hard she could not close her mouth and with the other I gripped her throat in a strangle hold. Then I surged down on her with my knees. To my surprise I felt a rib go – I did it again. I felt her relax, a sort of letting go, although she was still struggling. At the same time I felt myself weakening similarly, and then it became a question as to which would give up first. Little by little her struggling ceased. My strength had outlasted hers.

"After what seemed an interminable passage of time I let go and tried to stand, calling to the pony boy that it was finished. He now screwed up his courage sufficiently to approach. Then the leopard began to gasp, and I saw that she might recover; so I asked the boy for his knife. He had thrown it away in his fear, but quickly found it, and I at last made certain that the beast was dead. As I looked at her later I came to the conclusion that what had saved me was the first shot I had fired when she went into the bush. It had hit her right hind foot. I think it was this broken foot which threw out the aim of her spring and made her get my arm instead of my throat. With the excitement of the battle still on me I did not realise how badly used up I was. I tried to shoulder the leopard, to carry it to camp, but was very soon satisfied to confine my efforts to getting myself to camp.

"When I came inside the 'zareba', my companions were at dinner before one of the tents. They had heard the shots and had speculated on the probabilities. They had decided that I was not in a mix-up with a lion or with the natives, but that I would have the enemy or the enemy would have me before they could get to me; so they continued their dinner. The fatalistic spirit of the country had prevailed. When I came within their range of vision, however, my appearance was quite sufficient to arrest attention, for my clothes were all ripped, my arm was chewed into an unpleasant sight, and there was blood and dirt all over me. Moreover, my demands for all the antiseptics in camp gave them something to do, for nothing was keener in my mind than that the leopard had been feeding on the diseased hyena that I had shot in the morning. To the practical certainty of blood poisoning from any leopard bite not quickly treated was added the certainty that this leopard's mouth was particularly foul with disease. While my companions were getting the surgical appliances ready, my boys were stripping me and dowsing me with cold water. That done, the antiseptic was pumped into every one of the innumerable tooth wounds until my arm was so full of the liquid that an injection in one drove it out of another. During the process I nearly regretted that the leopard had not won. But it was applied so quickly and so thoroughly that it was a complete case.

"Later in the evening they brought the leopard in and laid it beside my cot. Her right foot showed where the first shot had hit her. The only other bullet that struck her was the last before she charged and that had creased her just under the skin on the back of the neck, from the shock of which she had instantly recovered.

"This encounter took place fairly soon after our arrival on my first trip to Africa. I have seen a lot of leopards since and occasionally killed one, but I have taken pains never to attempt it at such close quarters again. In spite of their fighting qualities I have never got to like or respect leopards very much. This is not because of my misadventure; I was hurt much worse by an elephant, but I have great respect and admiration for elephants. I think it is because the leopard has always seemed to me a sneaking kind of animal, and also perhaps because he will eat carrion even down to a dead and diseased hyena. A day or two before my experience with the leopard someone else had shot a hyena near our camp and had left him overnight. The next morning the dead hyena was lodged fiteen feet from the ground in the crotch of the tree at some distance from where he was killed. A leopard, very possibly my enemy, had dragged him along the ground and up the tree and placed him there for future use. While such activities cannot increase one's respect for the taste of leopards, they do give convincing evidence of the leopard's strength, for the hyena weighs at least as much as the leopard."